Kaitangata Twitch

MARGARET MAHY
Kaitangata Twitch

ALLEN&UNWIN

First published in 2005

Copyright © Margaret Mahy 2005

All rights reserved. No part of this book may be reproduced or transmitted
in any form or by any means, electronic or mechanical, including
photocopying, recording or by any information storage and retrieval
system, without prior permission in writing from the publisher.
The *Australian Copyright Act 1968* (the Act) allows a maximum of one chapter
or ten per cent of this book, whichever is the greater, to be photocopied by any
educational institution for its educational purposes provided that the
educational institution (or body that administers it) has given
a remuneration notice to Copyright Agency Limited (CAL) under the Act.

Allen & Unwin
83 Alexander Street
Crows Nest NSW 2065
Australia
Phone: (61 2) 8425 0100
Fax: (61 2) 9906 2218
Email: info@allenandunwin.com
Web: www.allenandunwin.com

National Library of Australia
Cataloguing-in-Publication entry:

Mahy, Margaret, 1936– .
Kaitangata twitch.

For children.
ISBN 1 74114 485 X.

I. Title.

NZ823.2

'Cannibal Isle' lyrics from a recording by George Formby; author not traced

Designed by Ellie Exarchos
Set in 11.7/17 pt Adobe Garamond by Midland Typesetters
Printed by McPherson's Printing Group

10 9 8 7 6 5 4 3 2

MARGARET MAHY's stories for children and teenagers are known and loved around the world. She is the author of 200 books ranging from funny and rumbustious to spooky and mysterious, and has twice won the Carnegie Medal, the UK award for best children's book. Margaret lives in Governor's Bay, New Zealand.

PART ONE

1

Flick! There it was again.

'*Need!*' whispered the voice. '*Need! Need!*'

Down on the beach, hauling the blue canoe from the family boathouse, Meredith listened, though it was not like ordinary listening. The words seemed to be welling up from deep inside her own head. She paused, frowning. Had she really heard those words or was it something she was making up? '*Need!*' urged the voice again. '*Danger! Danger!*' it said . . . it almost sang, but in a muffled and struggling way, as if the song were coming out of a mouth filled with moss. Then the voice chanted an answer to some question she had not asked. '*Need! Feed! Need! Feed!*'

Meredith stood, waiting and listening, but whatever it was had said all there was to say. So she bent once more and pushed the canoe out into the sly ripples that were licking the edge of the drowsy, late-spring land. *What am I doing here?* she asked herself as she began paddling, though it was a strange question, because she was doing what she often did on early Sunday mornings . . . what she had been planning to do as she went to bed the night before. *But is it morning? Why don't I remember waking up? Or getting dressed? Or anything?*

The donkeys lined up along the fence above the zigzag track, and began braying, asking a question, and then immediately answering it themselves. (*Hee? Haw! Hee? Haw!*) Smooth ripples curved away from the prow of the canoe, and the canoe, perhaps listening to the donkeys' question, seemed to be writing an answer of its own, an answer which vanished into the sea before it could be properly read. Meredith paddled on.

At last the canoe ran softly and grittily onto Shelly Beach, one of the seven little beaches that circled the island of Kaitangata. These beaches were separated from each other by fingers of rock, all pointing at different angles out to sea. Though the rounded western end of the island was blanketed by early-morning fog, the sharp eastern end was bright with light from an early morning sun . . . or was it afternoon? What time of day *was* it? The strange light seemed to be seeping up out of the land rather than falling on it from above. Meredith blinked and thought she must look for the sun properly – but in a minute.

Hee? Haw! Hee? Haw! The donkey voices were asking and answering.

Meredith headed towards the eastern end of the island, crossing one little beach then scrambling across rocks to the next one. She knew them all well, the four beaches on the south side and three on the north, and walked confidently over sand and thick drifts of broken shells, past sticks, sodden pine cones, plastic bottles and beercans tossed out of boats by weekend sailors, the skeleton of a fish pecked almost clean by gulls, a glove made of yellow rubber. Meredith was always surprised just how many rubber gloves washed up at the head of the bay. Shredded plastic bags punctuated the clumps of seaweed with harsh commas of blue and scarlet, and a black sandal made an exclamation mark at the end of whatever sentence the tide had written on the sand.

At last Meredith reached the eastern end of the island, picked her way around the familiar rocks, and found herself looking along the northern coast – three beaches and then the mist again. *Hee? Haw! Hee? Haw!* cried the donkey voices, which was strange, for she could not remember ever hearing them from this side of the island before.

Hadn't it had been something like sunlight a minute ago? So why did it suddenly seem so late? And not just late but *strangely* late, thought Meredith, frowning. The sky was clear and intensely blue, but there suddenly seemed to be something threatening about the curious deepness of that blue. Then she saw that since she'd been there last, someone had put up signs and *named* the beaches. HAND BEACH said the nearest sign – white printing on blue, exactly like the street signs in the new Trident Cove development. *A Marriott Carswell sign!* thought Meredith. Marriott Carswell. For years that name had suggested power and money, and yesterday he had been elected to the local council. Now it seemed he was out on Kaitangata too, labelling and dividing up her private world. Looking ahead to the second beach, she thought she could make out another sign beyond the next pointing finger of rock, while even further away, where the third beach began . . . but then Meredith forgot the signs.

Far ahead of her, in the distant mist stood a crowd of waiting people, dark and faceless. One figure stood in front of the others, poised as if patiently waiting to give a speech or offer a gift. Though Meredith could not be sure, she had the strangest feeling that it might be holding a bunch of flowers . . . the sort of flowers that brides carry, or that little children present to the wives of visiting prime ministers.

Who were they, those dim, waiting people? Who could possibly be standing there in this odd, brassy light on the empty island of Kaitangata? Meredith stepped off the rock and onto the sand. Immediately, something seized her ankle. Looking down, she saw the fingers of a pink rubber glove gripping her leg. She tried to kick it away, but the raw pink fingers tightened horribly, and then – then the whole beach flexed itself in front of her. It was as if that seemingly empty glove was really a hand, powered by a secret muscle running the whole length of the beach.

She screamed. Sand seemed to fall away around her, as if the island were opening a mouth. (*Flick! 'Feed!'* demanded that voice.) 'Help me! Help me!' she called, waving at the distant figures, but none of them stirred. Now she was chest-deep, then chin-deep, in sand, sticks and shells, struggling, writhing, as she felt other hands tightening on her, tugging her down, down and further down. One of her arms, somehow angled over her head, flapped in the air like a disjointed wing, while the other was jammed to her side by the heavy, wet sand. Struggle as she might, she was being drawn into the very stuff of the island.

She opened her mouth to scream again but wet sand forced its way up her nose and over her head, throttling her there, under the surface of Kaitangata. She was about to become part of the island for ever. And then . . .

And then Meredith woke up.

She was not on the island. She was not in her bed, either. She was kneeling on the window seat in the familiar, family sitting room, wearing her pyjamas, but with her new birthday binoculars dangling around her neck. Through the window in front of her she could see an old moon outlining Kaitangata in silver.

As she tried to empty the last of the nightmare out of her head, the whole world shuddered. This was not a dream-shivering. The ornaments on the mantelpiece behind her set up a frantic staccato rattling, the tongs and poker hanging by the fireside clanged against each other. Meredith saw the moonlit floor twisting as if two lines of ripples, running under the floor rugs, were coming at her from two directions at once and colliding under the window seat, which bucked as if it were trying to get rid of her. Two family photographs toppled softly forward into the fireplace. Then the ornaments stopped their frantic dancing. The world relaxed and grew still once more.

Meredith buried her face in the cushions, allowing

alternating ripples of panic and relief to wash over her. The relief grew stronger and stronger, driving the panic away. A bad dream – but only a dream. An earthquake – but only a little one. She stood, picked up the fallen photographs and placed them tenderly back on the shelf above the fireplace, then wound her way upstairs to bed. In the end, after making a small bed-earthquake of her own, tossing and turning, she *did* sleep . . . she *must* have slept . . . because she woke up in an ordinary way, without any further dreams – no dreams she was able to remember, anyhow. Even if she had remembered them, her father's voice might have hunted them out of her head and into the dissolving light of day.

2

'Of course he will ruin it. He'll ruin the whole bay!' Mr Skerritt cried, pacing from sitting room to kitchen and back again. 'They say he's got quite a mansion just out of Sydney. Why doesn't he run his wretched empire from Australia and leave us alone?'

Meredith, who was on her way downstairs, saw her wild, tall, craggy father come stalking out of the kitchen, only to stand, hesitating, as if he wanted to go in every direction at once.

'I mean, look what he's already done to Old Creek,' he ordered the sitting room, and Meredith decided to do exactly as her father said, even if he was really talking to himself. The binoculars were on the little table beside the couch, and, picking them up, Meredith stared across the bay towards the inlet that had once been called Old Creek. She could make out gingery scars of raw, volcanic soil scraped free of bush and grass and the distant glint of new surfaces – new glass, new tin, new paint – seeming to dissolve out of nothing.

'Of course we have to call it Trident Cove these days, don't we?' her father was exclaiming. 'And what about that great wall they're putting up along the roadside? Do they think that the people who are moving in there need to be *protected* from the rest of us? Well, take it from me, *they're* the pollution, not us.'

Meredith swept the binoculars around Old Creek then past it to Kaitangata, focusing on the very top, where grey knuckles of rock broke through the soil and grass. Hundreds of years ago the island had clenched an inner fist and punched up towards the sky. One day, if she was secret and sly enough, she might actually see ancient grey fingers unfold and . . . and snatch at seagulls, perhaps, or make some rude, mocking sign at the new houses of Old Creek which she must now call Trident Cove.

'Dad—' she began, but her father was in a lecturing mood, not a listening one.

'Marriott Carswell!' he exclaimed again, somehow making the name sound like a whole argument, nodding his head and utterly agreeing with himself as he spoke. 'Why has he come back to torment us? He won't be happy, you know – he just won't be happy – until he's turned the whole bay into a city suburb. And then *he'll* be able to move out and live in some unruined place across the Tasman because he'll have all the profit from ruining ours!'

As he began pacing the room again, Pudding, the big dog, half-labrador, half-poodle, sat up hopefully, thinking a walk might be in the offing. She was a simple dog and easily fooled. The other dog, Pie, smaller but cleverer, cocked his ears, but did not bother to lift his head from his paws. He simply lay there looking rather like the head of a ginger mop.

'Now he's on the council there'll be no stopping him,' said Mr Skerritt, suddenly slumping into the old green chair, which creaked and sagged a little to the left.

'Dad, you've said that ten times already.'

'Someone's got to say it, and *keep* saying it. We can't all have the fun of being dreamers like you.' He sat up. 'Have you done your music practice?' he asked.

At that moment Rufus, Meredith's younger brother, burst in through the door from the verandah, all ears and enthusiasm, followed by their mother and his good friend Allan Ponty. Mrs Skerritt walked up behind her husband's chair, pushed red curls away from the bald spot at the back of his head and planted a smacking kiss in the middle of it. Mr Skerritt was not comforted.

'Don't you *care?*' he cried, ducking sideways, and hastily stroking the hair back over his bald spot.

'Of course I do,' said Mrs Skerritt, just a little wearily. 'But I can't think of anything new to say. Because – face up to it – Marriott's been elected. That's democratic process at work isn't it, and we're all supposed to approve of democracy.'

'But he'll ruin the place!' cried Mr Skerritt.

'Dear, it's *his* land,' Mrs Skerritt said with a sigh. 'He's a Carswell *and* a Wittwood too. Right? And those families were battling the gorse and the long dry summers for years before we moved out here.'

'Carswells probably *planted* that gorse,' Mr Skerritt said. If he had been a cat, Meredith thought, he would have been flattening his ears against his skull.

'It's just a pity from our point of view that Marriott's such a natural exploiter,' said Mrs Skerritt. 'But why should he care about the Bay in the way that we do? I don't think he enjoyed living here when he was a kid, and by now he'll be a real city man. A lot of people are impressed with his international wheeler-dealer image.'

'Dad says Mr Carswell's got a good sense of humour,' said Allan Ponty shyly.

'Oh, Marriott can laugh all right!' said Mr Skerritt. 'Laugh all the way to the bank.'

'He didn't laugh much when he was at school,' said Mrs Skerritt. 'Remember?' (She was raising her voice a little.) 'You other boys were rough on him at times. Anyhow, all the land on this side of the bay is still designated "agricultural". So don't tear yourself to bits over things until you need to, darling! It may never happen.' She did not sound particularly hopeful, Meredith noticed.

Mr Skerritt was not pacified.

'Now he's on the council he'll have access to that new District Scheme they keep promising. He'll get them to reclassify everything he owns as "residential". And then he'll subdivide! Great heavens, *McDonald's* will probably move in.'

'McDonald's!' Rufus was excited for the first time. 'Good one! But not right *here*!' he added quickly, catching his father's rolling eye. 'Not next to *us*! At the head of the bay, beside the pub! Or over by Old Creek, I mean Trident Cove,' he added slyly. He often tried to keep family arguments going, just for the excitement of it all.

Out in the kitchen someone opened the fridge door. Dogs and boys turned in the direction of the sound.

'Did you feel the earthquake last night?' yelled Kate. Meredith could hear her rustling and rattling, scavenging for food.

'Earthquake?' exclaimed Rufus. 'What? That old Kaitangata twitch?'

'Yeah! Woke me up,' said Allan importantly.

'Kate, don't empty the fridge,' Mrs Skerritt called quickly. 'It's going to be lunchtime soon.'

'Plee-eeease!' wailed Kate. 'I'm *starving*.'

'I missed an earthquake,' Rufus cried. 'Did *you* feel it, Merry?'

'I felt something, but by this morning I thought I must've dreamed it,' Meredith answered vaguely.

'Typical!' said Rufus scornfully. 'She dreams all the time. She used to walk in her sleep,' he told Allan, looking at Meredith with a mixture of pride and envy.

'It wasn't a *big* earthquake,' said Allan in a comforting voice. 'Just the same old twitch.' And he rocked his right hand backwards and forwards, illustrating the earthquake's movement.

'A sign of *doom*,' cried Rufus, making his voice echo from the back of his mouth. Then he clutched his throat and staggered around the room 'Urrrrgh!'

'More likely a sign of Marriott Carswell being elected to the council,' Kate called from the kitchen in a muffled voice. She was enjoying a private, pre-lunchtime feast in there, even though she had been told not to eat anything. Rufus nudged Allan, and, when Mrs Skerritt wasn't looking, the two boys edged out to scavenge for themselves.

'Dad, why do we call earthquakes Kaitangata twitches?' asked Meredith.

'Local joke!' said her father, as, out in the kitchen, the fridge door opened for a second time.

Kate wandered in, eating a cold sausage. She was sixteen, a grown-up really, with her mother's fair hair and dark eyes. But whereas Mrs Skerritt's hair was scraped back into an untidy ponytail, Kate's floated around her in a cloud of pale gold. As she walked through a patch of sunlight, this floating hair became a glittering net, turning her into an illustration from a book of fairy tales, or a science-fiction diagram of an electronic field.

'Dad,' Kate said. 'Marriott Carswell doesn't own the whole bay. If he really tries to ruin things for us, couldn't the rest of us gang up on him, and make him back off?'

'Support at last!' responded Mr Skerritt, sending an approving glance in Kate's direction. 'Right! We need to *organise*. Some voters might be blind sheep, but there are plenty of us who can work out what's just around the corner.'

Meredith thought of saying something, and then decided she might as well save her breath. Kate and Mr Skerritt had a way of coming out with whatever it was the other one was about to say, which closed them in a world of two. Perhaps it was because Kate had been an only child for five years, or perhaps, thought Meredith, you could inherit views of the world just as you could inherit golden hair.

'Music practice, Meredith,' her mother reminded firmly, meaning it. Meredith put the binoculars on the window ledge. She had heard enough and seen enough to go on with. And, like her dreams, her music had surprises in it . . . surprises that even her family did not know about. Indeed, it sometimes seemed to Meredith that her dreaming and her music melted into each other, one making the other stronger.

3

In the beginning Meredith and Rufus had begun taking dancing lessons together, but Rufus had quickly turned out to be much the better dancer. Meredith had gone on to take piano lessons ('Right hand, left hand . . . don't *thump* the keys, Meredith'). Sitting at the piano, she felt she was getting closer to finding just what it was she really wanted to do. But there ahead of her, was Kate – always Kate – older and officially musical, standing in the doorway and shouting, 'Haven't you finished yet? I've got to practise too, you know.'

At school Meredith was part of a recorder group ('Squeak! Squeak! Squeak!' yelled Rufus, thumping at her bedroom door as he went by) and then when she was about ten her father came home, looking almost shy, yet secretly pleased with himself. He had bought her a flute.

'You're really good at the recorder,' he told her.

'I think you should try something with a bit more . . . more substance.' The flute worked well for Meredith. Now she and Kate could be partners rather than rivals for piano time. They played duets together while their parents sat side by side, their arms around one another, listening proudly. ('Thump! Thump! Squeak! Squeak!' yelled Rufus, leaping and spinning across the room behind them.)

A year ago Meredith had been walking on her own along the beach below the Zigzag, kicking stones and making up half-songs under her breath, when she heard faint, lonely music coming out of nowhere. Round and mellow, it was the sort of sound a full moon might make if it decided to sing. And there was the moon, lifting up over the hill like a magical pumpkin, flicking the ripples of the sea with fingers of light. The sound went on in a wandering way, feeling almost like part of the evening, part of the air.

Meredith stepped around a projecting rock, a remnant outflow from the old volcano that millions of years ago had made the crater that was now their harbour. There, sitting on a log on the sand, was her great-uncle from down the road, Lee Kaa, playing on a saxophone. It curved down in front of him like an upside-down question mark.

Lee saw her almost at once, and stopped playing. He waved a hand at her.

'Hello, cuzzy!' he said. All relations were 'cuzzy' to Lee. It saved him having to remember names.

'Keep on playing,' Meredith said. Lee Kaa grinned and played again, inventing a mellow sound that rose and fell, wound in on itself and then straightened out again as he went along. Meredith listened.

'Have a turn,' Lee said at last.

'Great!' said Meredith, eager to make that mysterious sound herself. But the saxophone felt awkward and heavy as she tried to find the best way of holding it, and the sound she made broke the spell. She spluttered . . . hooted . . . then she and Lee both laughed.

'Not too bad for a first time, mind you,' Lee said. 'You've even got a feel for the fingering.'

'I play the flute,' said Meredith. 'It's different, but it helps. There's a lot more stretch to the saxophone, though.'

'Keep on trying and you'll soon get the hang of it,' said Lee Kaa. 'Hey! No reason why you shouldn't have something from our side, is there?'

He lifted his head and listened.

'Me-e-eredith!' someone was calling from far down the beach behind them. 'Me-e-eredith!'

'Someone's mum! She's looking for you,' Lee said unnecessarily, and walked with her back down the beach to meet her mother and Rufus taking their own kind of evening walk, with Mrs Skerritt strolling along looking at the moon, and Rufus leaping and cartwheeling like a spirit of salt and seaweed.

Every now and then, on the long evenings during that particular summer, when she wasn't hanging out with her best friends Sharon Ponty and Kirsten Appleton, Meredith would wander down to the beach, with sharp slopes rising on her right, and sea and the dark shape of Kaitangata on her left. Every now and then, Lee Kaa would be there, sitting on his log and playing the saxophone in the last sunlight or under an early moon. He always let Meredith have a turn and, slowly, she found she really was getting the hang of it.

'Better and better,' said Lee. 'Long way to go, but better.'

Back at home Meredith said, 'Mum, I want to play the saxophone.' Her mother gave her a sudden sideways look, sharp, amused and knowing.

'You've been listening in on old Lee Kaa,' she said immediately. 'Great, isn't he?'

Her father ran his fingers through his red hair, making his curls stand on end.

'But what about the flute!' he exclaimed. 'You're doing so well. You and Kate sound wonderful together.'

Meredith did not argue. Deep down she liked the idea that she was doing something . . . not outside family life, exactly, but somehow off to one side of it. If she took official lessons she would probably have to follow the notes written in lines on a page of music. She would have to put up with Rufus banging on her door and hooting. There was a lot to be said for playing every now and then in the evening with Lee Kaa as her teacher and her only listener . . . unless you counted Kaitangata, that island lying like a secret, strange tear on the moonlit cheek of the harbour.

4

'Well, I reckon the old man's going round the twist,' said Rufus, talking tough.

Meredith looked over her shoulder at the door to the sitting room, then made a hissing sound as she slotted a blue dish into the draining rack.

'That's steam coming out of his ears,' she explained.

'I mean it'd be *great* having McDonald's on this side of the hill,' Rufus went on, drying a spoon with far more care than he needed to because he wasn't really thinking about it. 'Mum's pretty good when it comes to gardening and donkeys, but she's not great at cooking – she *burns* a lot because she's always running outside to water something . . . so if we could just shoot along and get a few Big Macs . . .'

'Even if there is a subdivision,' said Meredith, 'it'll be ages before they build a McDonald's here. You'll have left school by then.'

Rufus looked grumpy at the prospect of having to wait so many years for junk food. He searched around for something else to complain about.

'And why don't we get a dishwasher?' he went on. 'A lot of really *good* people have them. Even forest-and-bird people who recycle stuff, and grow herbs, and . . . and eat wholemeal bread.'

'You know why we don't have one,' said Meredith. 'Mum and Dad have got *us* to wash up for them.'

'They'd get one if they had to wash up themselves,' said Rufus. 'I've had more practice at washing and drying than anything else in my life.'

'You're not just drying that spoon,' Meredith said severely. 'You're *polishing* it.'

'I mean, I *like* living here,' Rufus went on, dropping the spoon hastily into the spoon drawer, 'but it takes ages to *get* anywhere. It wouldn't hurt if the city was just a bit closer . . .'

Kate, coming into the kitchen, overheard him.

'Don't you dare to wish for anything like that,' she said fiercely. 'The bay's just great the way it is.'

'But you go to *college*,' said Rufus. 'You get into town *five* times a week. Kids like Allan and me have to hang around here, day after day, day after day . . . *bor*ing, except for when Mum takes me to dancing lessons and the supermarket. Same old people, same old blah-blah-blah. There's nothing to *do*.'

'We can paddle out to Kaitangata,' said Meredith. 'We've got canoes.'

'Oh, big deal!' Rufus cried. 'Canoes! What if I want to go somewhere *trendy* – to video parlours or to one of those skateboard places?'

Kate groaned.

'A video parlour! What a loser!'

'You know what? You're turning into a grown-up,' Rufus pulled a face, mimed a woman's curves with his hands, then minced around the room, walking on tiptoe as if he were wearing high heels. 'Dear oh dear! Fun is so *bad* for kids,' he said in a high-pitched voice. Then he flopped back into being himself again. 'Nothing ever happens here,' he said, mournfully. '*Bor*ing!'

'You're the boring one,' said Kate, sliding out of the kitchen quickly. They all had homework, but Kate's was so serious that she was let off dishwashing duties.

'Anyway,' Rufus went on, 'when we're grown up, *I'll* hang out in the city, dancing and going to cafés and video parlours, and you can paddle around in your canoe, dream, dream, dream.' His expression changed. 'Hey – have you *had* any good dreams lately?' he asked.

Rufus loved to hear about Meredith's dreams. She had stranger dreams than anyone else in the family, and she remembered them in great detail, and could tell them like stories after she was awake. Through inventing and dreaming, asking and answering, she and Rufus had once made up a whole dishwashing serial – a true soap opera – that went on night after night.

Now Meredith scoured the bottom of a frying pan, plunging her fingers deep into the tangled, metallic threads of the new pot-scrub.

'The enchantress has a new enemy,' she said, in her storytelling voice. 'His name is Karrykot Marswell, and he uses the heads of gnomes to scrub out his pots.' She swung her hand, the pot-scrub like a tiny head covered in wiry golden curls right in front her brother's face. Rufus yelped and stepped back. As she acted out this little horror moment, Meredith felt her face turning tight and chilly, as if it had truly become the face of a merciless enchantress.

'Did you really *dream* that, or are you just making it up?' Rufus asked.

Meredith let the enchantress expression fade away, and went back to work on the frying pan, inventing aloud as she did so.

'The enchantress is more powerful than she used to

be. These days she has a voice like a saxophone. And she has the power to *summon*. She calls, and you *have* to come.'

'No, I don't,' said Rufus.

'Yes, you do,' said Meredith, making her voice deep, mysterious and a little threatening, 'because the enchantress wears a summoning ring.'

She held up her hand, and now something gleamed on her middle finger. Rufus's mouth dropped open slightly. Then he shut it firmly again.

'One ring to bind them all,' he said, for over the winter the family had read *The Lord of the Rings* aloud, and Rufus felt he knew all about rings of power.

Meredith laughed.

'One ring to *scrub* them all,' she said, for the ring she was showing him was a single, golden, curling wire that had detached itself from the pot-scrub and cunningly twisted itself around her finger. 'The enchantress has power over dirty dishes. She never, ever has to wash up, because she has the power of call and command. You know how people – the bossy ones out there' (she pointed in the direction of the sitting room) 'say "Meredith, will you come . . ."' (Meredith made her voice spooky and remote) '". . . will you co-o-ome and clear these dishes off the table!" or "Just stop arguing and do those dishes, Rufus!" Well, the power of call and command is in this ring. Whoever you call *has* to do the dishes for you. Even Kate, if I called her. Kate! Kate! Ka-a-te!' she wailed three times.

'It's not much of a power,' said Rufus. 'Not like striking enemies dead, or being able to project yourself through space.'

The kitchen phone rang shrilly. Kate came rushing into the room.

'It'll be for me,' she said.

'Nick Chambers,' cried Rufus mockingly, dancing out of reach.

'Go on! Get lost!' yelled Kate.

'We've still got to wipe down,' Rufus pointed out virtuously.

'Get lost!' Kate repeated, holding her hand across the mouthpiece of the receiver. '*I'll* wipe down. OK? Out! Or I'll wipe *you*!'

'Is Nick a proper boyfriend?' Rufus asked Meredith as they went through into the sitting room. 'Or is she just practising?'

Meredith shrugged. But Rufus suddenly turned on her, flinging out arms like sudden wings.

'Hey! It worked!' he exclaimed.

'What worked?'

'Your ring! You held it up, and called Kate, and she came rushing in to wipe down. She'd never do that unless she was under a spell. Use it first thing tomorrow and she'll do all the breakfast dishes!'

'Wow!' said Meredith, looking at her finger. 'I'll save this ring for ever.'

'I'll get one too,' said Rufus.

'You can't just take any old pot-scrub wire and make a magic ring out of it,' objected Meredith. 'The wire has to choose you. And it chose me because I can dream power into it. I'm the family dreamer. You're just the family dancer.'

'Dream!' she said silently to herself. 'Call! Command! Be the enchantress!' And, drawing herself up, she felt her body fill with a power that came so quickly and easily it astonished her. But perhaps, thought Meredith, the power was not really hers.

Flick! There it was again. That sound that was not only a sound but a heartbeat too. And, as that *Flick!* twitched in her head once more, it was as if a finger (she had a picture of a *child's* finger for some reason) had crooked and beckoned, and something deep in her brain had trembled in reply. But then she told herself to forget about the *Flick!* and forget the ring, too, because, after all, being the enchantress with the ring of golden wire – an enchantress who could play the saxophone – was just one of those games that make washing up more interesting. There was nothing real about that enchantress, nothing at all.

'Homework!' her mother was calling.

'It's Friday,' cried Rufus. 'No school tomorrow.'

'Get it over and done with and then you'll have the weekend to yourselves,' said Mrs Skerritt. 'I hate that mad scramble on Sunday night.'

'Dishes and then homework,' wailed Rufus. 'Slavery!'

'It would only be slavery if you'd had to cook your own dinner,' his mother said.

So it was homework, followed by family reading, then bed, and at last a drifting into sleep.

5

Opening her eyes sharply next morning, Meredith saw Saturday taking over the world. A faint golden blush crept across her ceiling, while shadows of leaves suddenly worked their way out of the wall beside her to dance a few inches from her nose.

Sitting up, she looked at her hands then bent her knees, patting them through the blanket. *All of me here!* she thought. *And it's Saturday.*

The night before, Meredith had decided to start her Saturday by paddling out to Kaitangata, climbing up to the very top of that punching fist, and standing on the clenched fingers of stone. She needed to remind herself (and the island too) that it was only an island, and that it did not hold her prisoner in the sand. After all, Kaitangata was her favourite lonely place in the entire world, and she wasn't going to let a nightmare ruin it for her.

Rolling over sideways and grabbing her jeans from the wobbly table beside her bed, she dressed quickly while those leaf-shadows trembled on the walls around her. Hearing her footsteps, the dogs whined and snuffled from behind the laundry door but she ignored them sternly, not wanting any company, not even the company of dogs, that particular morning.

Six o'clock . . . and outside, there was a faint movement in the air, a movement too small to be called a wind just yet. Out beyond the line of green fur marking the edge of the lawn (otherwise known as the End of the World), the tide was full in; the water shone as if the softly stirring morning air had carefully polished it. The hills of the bay and the knotted hump of Kaitangata rose out of that glass, but also hung, reflected, below it. Perhaps the island of her dreaming was that other, looking-glass island.

'Hey!' called a voice. Rufus was out on the verandah, pulling on yesterday's blue sweater.

'I'm not doing anything interesting,' Meredith said quickly, sliding a look back over her shoulder. 'Only canoeing over to Kaitangata.'

'Me too,' he cried immediately.

'Last night you said it was boring,' she reminded him.

'I'm having the blue canoe!' Rufus cried, leaping from

the verandah without bothering about the steps. He hit the ground running.

'Whoever gets there first has the blue one,' Meredith cried back, launching herself across the slope of lawn and onto the Zigzag.

'My turn! My turn!' Rufus yelled, and he kept on yelling at Meredith's elbow, even though he didn't stand any chance of passing her. The Zigzag, cutting down between dense scrub on high banks, was so narrow that it was almost impossible to crowd past anyone running ahead of you. All the same, Meredith sped on as fast as she dared, swinging left, swinging right ... left again, right again, and sliding around the sharp corners, because the sliding and swinging was good fun. She burst out onto the beach, well ahead of Rufus, and leaped towards the tumbledown Skerritt boathouse. By the time Rufus caught up with her, still panting 'My turn! My turn!' as if the words were a rhythm to run to, Meredith had grabbed the loop on the prow of the blue canoe and was hauling it out onto the sand.

'Mi-hi-hi!' Rufus gasped, but he didn't try and pull the canoe away from Meredith. Instead he slipped into the boathouse to grab the yellow canoe – the second-best one.

'Wear a lifejacket!' Meredith reminded him sternly.

Rufus sighed. 'Do I *have* to?'

'Mum'll ask,' Meredith said, unhooking her own lifejacket from the boathouse wall.

'Mole and Rat never wore lifejackets,' grumbled Rufus. 'Swallows and Amazons didn't.'

'Yeah, but they didn't have mothers,' said Meredith. 'Well, Mole and Rat didn't. Anyway, they were old-fashioned.' And Rufus, who hated the thought of being old-fashioned, fell silent.

'The mothers of the Swallows and Amazons made them a tent . . . *made–them–a–tent*,' he began again, a little later, fastening his jacket and repeating the words as if a home-made tent was something he found it impossible to believe in. 'And they made themselves a flag, and did sailing against the wind and stuff like that. But no lifejackets!'

'All the crews in the America's Cup race wore lifejackets,' Meredith said, pushing herself off with the paddle. She longed to be skimming swift, silent and above all solitary across the shallow sea while the island slowly swelled before her, filling her head with strangeness. The true mysteriousness of sea and island would never come to her this morning, with Rufus shouting and splashing behind her. That mystery, like Lee Kaa's wandering saxophone sound, belonged to solitude.

And now someone else was shouting. It was Kate this

time, Kate jogging along the beach towards the boathouse, hair flopping as she ran. And Kate had let the dogs out, too. Pudding was already chest-deep in the water while Pie raced up and down the beach like a mop-head given magical life, wanting to be out there with the leaders but unwilling to swim. The lonely morning was suddenly crowded to its very edges with family life.

'She's mad because you've got the blue canoe,' said Rufus with satisfaction. 'Why is the blue canoe the best one?' he asked a moment later.

Meredith found she could not quite remember why. 'It's just the one we all want,' she said. 'It's the biggest, I suppose.' Directly ahead of her, the island, half dream, half sea-animal, basked and waited.

The water below the dipping paddle turned a darker green. They were now over the deepest part of the channel that ran between island and mainland. But it soon grew shallow again, and at last they glided in at Shelly Beach, mud giving way to sand, then sand to shell. The canoes grated to a gritty standstill. Meredith leaped out; Rufus leaped out. Together they pulled both canoes across tidelines of sticks and thick, kelpy seaweed which smelt of salt and gleamed with occasional stars of water-washed glass. Kate was coming after them in the green canoe – the oldest one. Even from a distance, Kate looked like a princess in a fairytale ... not a palace princess (she was too brown for that) but one who had escaped from some wicked stepmother and had been surviving with her own sort of happy richness out in the wild.

Meredith's eyes wandered to the world above and beyond Kate's head. She could see the roof of their own house among its trees, with the donkey paddocks to the left, and above it pieces of the road which ran behind their house before curving down around the donkey paddocks towards the beach. A sleek, scarlet Saturday car showed briefly on this curve, then disappeared behind a huge boathouse – a Carswell boathouse, for the land on the other side of the road was all Carswell land and even though Marriott lived in the city and spent a lot of time over in Sydney, being a clever businessman he owned two expensive boats much newer and smarter than anything the Skerritts could afford. (Not, as Mr Skerritt pointed out over and over again, that they would ever want noisy boats like those. The Skerritts were yachtspeople not speedsters.) Powerlines, beautiful as spiderwebs at that hour in the morning, swung from pole to pole in huge, thin curves of light, as they swept majestically down, bringing electricity to the Carswell boathouse.

On the upper side of the road, more Carswell land rose, slowly at first, then rather more sharply, finally becoming bush-clad slopes that overlooked everything the Skerritts owned. Meredith tried to imagine this hillside covered in houses, tried to imagine strangers on new balconies and verandahs, lying in recliner chairs or under bright sun-umbrellas and staring curiously down at the Skerritt barbecues or watching them struggle to file the hoofs of unwilling donkeys.

'Let's climb,' she suggested, beginning to cast along the beach for the beginning of a faint, familiar track that wound to the top of the island.

'Oh no! Not climbing!' said Rufus, disgusted with any plan that involved inching between gorse bushes. 'Let's go *round*!'

'*I'm* climbing,' Meredith persisted, and she clambered up at (more or less) the place where only yesterday afternoon she had imagined seeing, through her birthday binoculars, something scramble and vanish.

'Hang on,' said Rufus, his eyes fixed on Kate in the green canoe, only a short distance now from Shelly Beach.

But Meredith, pushing between the woody legs of old gorse bushes, left the beach, her brother and her sister behind her. At last she was alone.

6

She knew just where she was going. She was following the remains of an old track. Gorse had grown so thickly around it that sometimes she had to crawl along on her hands and knees, or flatten herself to slide between tough, spiked stems which thrust fierce elbows upwards and sideways. The ground was thick with dried and fallen prickles which jabbed painfully. Even here it was hard to be completely alone. From the harbour beyond came the sound of two speeding boats, one far away and the other much closer. Someone was taking the advantage of a full tide to skim scornfully around Kaitangata, disturbing the echoes and the crabs.

Meredith came to a place where she could stand up, but walking was still not easy. She climbed in a this-way that-way dance of small tortures . . . turned right, drew in her stomach, spun left quickly, offering as little of her skin to the gorse as she could. Even the soft new growth stung her legs and forearms; sometimes she pinched it aside, and curved herself around it, but almost always it found some way to strike at her.

Suddenly she stopped. The track in front of her tumbled into a gaping hole – a cave-in or underrunner. Meredith couldn't help thinking it was like a new mouth the island had opened at her. She edged around it as if the island might really try to snap her up.

Coming out of the last of the gorse was like coming from one world into another. Here she was free, under a wide sky. Meredith suddenly felt she had become God's eye, taking in the hillsides, the bright wink of Trident Cove, and the way the bay opened its arms widely towards the open sea, as if to embrace it and become true ocean at last. *Maybe that's what it really wants*, Meredith thought. *Maybe it longs to be true ocean.*

'Once upon a time . . .' she began, speaking aloud, and then fell silent. Just being here was a story beyond words.

A great rock had partly broken through the soil almost at her feet. She stepped onto it, then onto another and then another. Wild thrift, its buds stained bright pink and purple, pushed out of cracks so bare of soil that the plants seemed to be growing from the rock itself.

There were foxgloves too, mostly past their best, with only a few bells left at the top of inclining stems. And then it was nothing but rocks and thrift. Meredith had reached the very top of the island. Now only the rocks were higher than she was, and rocks could be climbed.

Using handholds her father had once shown her, Meredith pulled herself towards the hollow where she planned to sit and stare. But as her eyes came level with that secret sitting place, she froze. Someone had been there before her. Someone had left her – what? A message? A clue?

In the hollow lay a bunch of flowers – not the sort of flowers that Meredith might have gathered herself, wandering around the island, not thrift and foxgloves, clover and grass-heads tied together with a thread of flax. This bunch could only be called a bouquet. In it were rosebuds just opening, love-in-a-mist (huge blue single eyes fringed with sparse green lashes), delicate white sprays and strangest of all, freesias, even though freesias in all bay gardens had stopped flowering weeks and weeks ago. The bouquet was carefully held in place by a paper frill and tied with white ribbons.

Meredith put out a hand – then drew it back, finding she could not bear to touch this lure. Something about it suggested danger.

Moving very slowly, Meredith stepped backwards and downwards, her feet finding the places they knew to be there. Halfway down, since she could not bear to go slowly any more, she simply let go with both feet and hands, and leaped backwards to the ground, staggering as she landed, scraping her leg on a rock, and falling forward at last on her hands and knees. One of the scrapes was deep enough to bleed. Big drops of blood ran down on bare soil, which soaked them up quickly – sucked them up greedily, Meredith thought.

Flick! Kaitangata said to her, '*Need! Need! Feed! Feed!*'

As the blood disappeared, becoming a mere stain on the sandy soil, something stirred in the island. There was a curious sound – the whole earth creaking, rocks gritting against one another. Meredith, still on all fours and clenching her teeth against pain, felt the world under her palms and knees rise, then fall, as if Kaitangata had secretly gasped for breath . . . or for more blood, perhaps. No one could tell. It was almost like an earthquake – almost like the Kaitangata twitch – but somehow she knew that this particular twist was all in her head. Out there, drenched in Saturday sunlight, the island was really perfectly still.

Stumbling to her feet, she set off at a limping run, not towards the track she had scrambled up by, but to another, clearer path, the one that people usually used if they wanted to climb to the top of the island. It was not any earthquake-fear that hounded her. It was the thought of those flowers set down like some sort of sacrifice on the stony dimple of the island's fist, and also the thought that somewhere, at some time, she had seen that exact bouquet before. Yet she was quite unable to remember where or when.

7

The path that Meredith was now following wound down towards the sharper eastern end of the island. She held her breath, stepping as quickly as she dared over the more crumbling pieces of the track, and then began to hear voices – Rufus, of course, somewhere down below and to her right, shouting 'Look! Look!', and a quiet, answering murmur, Kate's voice. Then she heard Rufus say 'There's someone there already,' in a flattened voice, as if he did not want to be heard.

Meredith burst through the trees and onto the rocks. The bay opened out in front of her like hands parting to set something free.

There was a man poised on rocks to her right. Meredith stared at him, startled, and he stared back at her.

'Surprise, surprise!' he said, sounding cheerful, but rather sarcastic too.

'He's talking to someone,' said Rufus's voice to her right, and then Rufus and Kate appeared.

Meredith was sure she had never actually seen this man before, yet there was something familiar about the short, springy hair curving down to a point in the centre of his forehead, and his funny, long, lopsided grin. Pie began barking and, after staring around in her usual dizzy fashion, Pudding barked too, just for the fun of making noise.

'Hey!' said the man. 'None of that!' He held out his hand to the dogs, who fell silent, suddenly obedient, and edged up to sniff him. On his little finger he wore a ring made of silver. Meredith could see it was carved in some way. Pudding stretched out her long nose cautiously and licked the fingers.

'Attack successfully subdued,' the man said.

'*We're* the ones who are being attacked,' Kate replied. Meredith was astonished at the hostility in her voice. 'You're the one who's ruining things around here. And it's not even your home. It's ours.'

'And who are "we"?' the man inquired. Then he looked at her sharply. His expression changed. 'OK! Don't bother answering. I can guess who you are.' His eyes shifted. He looked at Rufus, then at Meredith and then at Kate again, carefully studying her golden hair and his eyes running up and down her long olive legs. 'Just let me point out that this isn't your land. It's mine.'

Of course! This was the face that had been looking down from small posters on local walls and telegraph poles for the last few weeks. This was the wicked magician who had turned Old Creek into Trident Cove, Marriott Carswell himself.

'We come here all the time,' Rufus explained, sounding surprised that someone could not know this.

'I'll just bet you do,' said Marriott Carswell. 'And then you go home and listen to your old man saying nasty things about me. Well, you need my permission to wander around this island, so get out of here right now.' He looked around as if he were suddenly measuring something no one else could see. 'There must be a few millionaires out there who'd love to own a place on an island,' he added thoughtfully.

'Millionaires like white sand, not mud and crabs,' muttered Meredith.

'But you can't actually *own* an island, can you?' said Rufus, sounding genuinely incredulous. 'Aren't they like beaches? No one can own *beaches*.'

'I think you'll find I own this one,' said Marriott Carswell levelly. 'You're nothing but trespassers.'

'We don't care,' said Kate in a chilly voice. 'Keep your boring little lump of grit. Come on, you kids!'

She swung round, and marched off. Meredith and Rufus followed her. Pudding and Pie dived ahead of them, as if they knew the way better than anyone else did.

'Hey! Do tell your mother you saw me,' Marriott Carswell called after them. The words were ordinary enough, the sort of thing you might write at the end of a letter, yet he seemed to give them an extra malevolent meaning. None of the children answered him. Within a few minutes they were all on Shelly Beach and making for their canoes.

8

'I absolutely, utterly *hate* that man,' said Kate, coming to a stop so suddenly that Meredith cannoned into her back and Rufus almost ran into Meredith's. 'I didn't like him before, but now I've met him I utterly hate him.'

'He wasn't as nasty as I thought he'd be, though,' said Rufus, sounding puzzled. 'He looked as if he enjoyed laughing! Boy, did you see that ring he was wearing? It was carved with two hands holding one another.'

'Dad's right,' said Kate fiercely. 'That man doesn't care about—' She waved her hand at the path ahead of them.

'He doesn't care about *gorse*?' said Rufus. 'Oh wow! Send for Batman!'

Kate glared at him.

'He could just ruin our home,' she cried. 'He could wipe out everything around us. Imagine looking out of our windows and seeing nothing but huge houses and marinas and speedboats.'

'We could look out of *other* windows,' argued Rufus.

'Our biggest, best windows look onto his land,' said Kate. 'And anyhow, he'll probably cover the hills behind us with houses, too. He's on the council now and he wants to subdivide the hills into lifestyle blocks. You know, big houses, a pony for the kids and six black sheep, so the mum can belong to the Coloured Wool Craft Group.'

'That isn't so bad, is it?' asked Rufus. 'I mean having sheep and a pony.'

'But the hills will be changed for ever,' cried Kate. 'This is our home – our *home*', she added, almost shouting the word at Rufus. 'Don't you *care*?'

'But isn't it greedy to want things to stay the same?' persisted Rufus. 'I mean,' he went on, struggling to get things clear, 'things must be – must be able to change or . . .' His voice faded and he looked around as if the end of his sentence might be hanging somewhere in the air around him.

'He mightn't be able to build on Kaitangata,' said Meredith. 'It's pretty crumbly. It's always falling in on itself – sort of eating itself from inside.' She thought of that new gaping mouth opened beside the track through the gorse.

'He'll find a way,' said Kate bitterly. 'Men like that always do. And it's not just the island. He'll want more.'

They scrambled into their canoes and set off home, with Pie sharing Meredith's canoe this time, and Pudding dog-paddling after them.

As they were tugging their canoes towards the boathouse again, Lee Kaa walked past them, carrying a sack. Lee's market garden, with its long glasshouses, was two bays further on, and he often began his Saturdays by walking all the way to the head of the bay and then back again, collecting seaweed for his compost heap.

'Hello, you lot!' he said. 'Been out on the water?'

'We've been over to Kaitangata,' Meredith said.

'You be careful, then,' he said. He was smiling, yet it seemed to Meredith that there was an edge of real warning in his voice.

'We were wearing lifejackets,' shouted Rufus, pleased with the chance to point out how faultless he had been.

'I mean be careful on Kaitangata,' said Lee, answering Rufus but looking at Meredith. 'It's fifty years since Shelly Gentry disappeared, and fifty's one of those numbers that seems as if it means something. People celebrate fifty and maybe islands do too. So watch out.'

For some reason the name Shelly Gentry brought a picture of the flowers laid secretly on the top of

Kaitangata's grey knuckle into Meredith's mind. She drove it out again, and found herself trying to remember exactly who Shelly Gentry had been. The name somehow suggested a sort of smudgy sadness. Hadn't there once been some accident? Some old calamity?

'It's the island that needs to watch out,' Kate was saying. 'Guess who was out there, skiting and grinning?'

Lee Kaa glanced back over his shoulder.

'Well, judging from the fact that I saw our local Mr Big had parked his red Jag on the road back there by his boathouse, I'd say you ran into Marriott Carswell.'

'He's talking about selling bits of Kaitangata to millionaires,' said Kate.

'He was just bullshitting,' cried Rufus. 'Millionaires don't want islands you can almost *paddle* to.'

'He wasn't!' Kate said, turning on Rufus impatiently. 'He'll find a way to make money by ruining it. *That's* what he was telling us. And he was really nasty. It wasn't so much what he said, as the way he said it.'

'Yeah, well,' said Lee Kaa. 'He just might be taking on a bit too much if he tried his development tricks on Kaitangata.'

Meredith was still thinking of the name 'Shelly Gentry'. The Kaitangata beach mightn't be called Shelly Beach just because of its shells.

'Who *was* Shelly Gentry?' she asked.

'Don't they bother to teach you history these days?' said Lee. He jerked his thumb back towards Kaitangata. 'A kid drowned. Well, probably drowned! Vanished, anyway. Vanished out on Kaitangata.'

'What happened to her?' Rufus asked.

'I told you!' said Lee. 'Disappeared on her birthday. There was a party over there on Shelly Beach. Kids everywhere having a good time. Then there was an earthquake, they say. And we had an earthquake ourselves the other day,' he went on, flicking the conversation out of the past and into the present as if it were all part of the same thing. 'The old Kaitangata twitch! First the twitch, and then the trouble!'

'Who says that?' asked Rufus.

'People!' said Lee vaguely, answering Rufus but looking at Meredith again.

'Coming up for a cup of tea?' Kate interrupted.

'Might call in on my way back,' said Lee. 'Tell your dad not to worry too much about Marriott.'

'We *have* to worry,' cried Kate hotly. 'He's a councillor now, isn't he, and a lot of other councillors are licking his boots, so he'll probably be able to grant himself permission to develop anything he wants to develop. And he wants to hurt *us* . . . our family. I could tell he does just from the way he looked at me . . . at *us*, that is. And also, he doesn't care what he does. I mean, look at the Creek across there, screaming every weekend with speedboats and jet-skis.'

Lee made a sound, half-snort, half-laugh.

'Katie, I'm on your side,' he said, 'but I remember a lot of things you don't. I remember how we old-timers had to get used to you lot,' he said.

The Skerritts had been about to move off up the Zigzag, but now Kate stopped, looking sharply at him. 'How did *we* change things?' she demanded.

'Roads!' Lee said. 'Roads came after you lot, like tame snakes. Then, of course, everyone else followed the roads: cars, motorbikes, the lot.'

'Well, roads . . .' began Kate, suddenly confused. 'We *have* to have roads.' And then she fell silent, frowning as if Lee had asked her a riddle.

'We could do without. We could ride over the hills on our *donkeys*,' cried Rufus, gleefully, sensing Kate's uncertainty. 'You could leave for school the night before and then get back—'

'Shut up!' said Kate. 'Anyhow, it's not the same. Donkeys are part of Nature.'

'See you on my way home, maybe,' said Lee, grinning.

Kate's face cleared. She grinned back.

'I don't care,' she said. 'We have to be miles better than dirty old Marriott Carswell.'

'I'm with you there,' Lee said. 'And I'd put my money on Kaitangata . . . if I was a betting man, that is.'

He winked, then walked off down the beach. Meredith, Rufus and Kate set off up the hill all thinking of breakfast. As they came out at the top of the Zigzag their father suddenly appeared on the verandah, leaped down the steps, (automatically avoiding the third one, the wobbly one), and onto the lawn in front of them. He flung out his arms and whirled around, as if he were Rufus, his red hair standing out almost like a wig.

'We were beginning to worry that you might be gone for good,' he cried. 'Your mother's been at me, telling me what a pain I've been with my moaning and groaning, so I've promised to reform and from now on it'll be all feasting and fun.'

And then, to prove it, he began to dance and sing.

'I've just come back from a cannibal isle
Called Hi-tiddly-hi-ti-ti Isle!
Tum tum tum tum . . .

'I forget the next bit . . . Oh yes.' He slicked his hand back over his head as he remembered a bit of the song he had lost.

*'On Hi-tiddly-hi-ti Island,
Everybody wears a smile.
On Hi-tiddly-hi-ti Island,
Everybody lives in style . . .'*

And then, because he had forgotten the words again, he sang 'Tra la la', jigging happily at the Edge of the World while behind him, on the verandah, Rufus joined in, dancing, as it happened, rather better than his father.

At the sound of this old, cheerful song, Meredith felt all strangeness and threat flow out of the day, and fun flow back into it. When ten minutes later she stole a passing, almost accidental glance at Kaitangata through her bedroom window, it looked altogether ordinary, just a lump of land with shallow water around it. Which was what it was, no doubt about it.

9

Flick!

Meredith scrambled out of the blue canoe and stood on the Kaitangata beach, looking up over the gorse to the clenched fist of the island. Once again she was bathed in that puzzling light and supposed, within her dream, that she might be dreaming.

'You again!' she said aloud. 'What do you want?'

'*Eat! Eat! Eat!*'

'Eat *what*?' Her voice seemed to run ahead of her down the beach, slipping over the seaweed and driftwood as if it expected her to follow it. 'Oh no!' she said. 'I'm not going there again. It was *me* you tried to eat last time.'

Flick!

'*Hungry!*'

And then she began to wake up, to find herself lying out on the verandah in the early summer morning.

By now Meredith felt she was becoming used to that voice. She looked around, wondering if she might even become used to waking up in some place other than her own bed. Certain dreams seemed to have the power to nudge her out into the world. She pulled herself onto all fours, feeling rather bruised after sleeping hard. She stretched upwards: she stretched sideways. Then she went inside to make herself an illegal pre-breakfast breakfast of noodles. She would take it up to her room, read as she ate it in bed and then come down later to wholesome stewed apple, organic muesli and home-made yoghurt. She felt she deserved comfort. And it *was* a Saturday morning, after all. No school. Bliss!

The phone in the sitting room rang sharply. The day woke up. Perhaps it had been having a dream of its own. Meredith could hear her father grumbling sleepily as he padded down the passage to answer it.

'Who?' she heard him say. '*What?*' There was silence while he listened. Then he began shouting again. 'I knew it! Didn't I *tell* you? Yes! No! I'll contact our local group! We'll have to organise – call a meeting, work out submissions. A protest – yes! Thanks for the info! No! Not too early! Never too early! Never too late! Bye for now!'

He slammed the phone down.

'What's wrong?' asked Meredith's mother. Her voice was both sleepy and worried at the same time.

'It's war,' he cried. 'Didn't I say . . . Haven't I been telling everyone—'

'Go on! Just tell me again,' Mrs Skerritt said, sounding wide awake now. 'Then we'll put on our tin helmets, bring the donkeys inside and dig up the front lawn.'

Meredith could hear her father take a deep breath.

'I told you I should have gone to that meeting last night,' he declared. 'That was Stafford Keys on the phone. The council produced that new District Scheme at last – sprang it on everyone – and under this scheme the entire Beckett block and all Wittwood land will be reclassified as "residential". Carswell must have had this all cooked up beforehand. Stafford says it's a really comprehensive document, not the sort of thing anyone slings together overnight. He says it would have taken months to come up with something like that. He was obviously working on it even before he was elected to the council.'

In the kitchen Meredith was dropping noodles into a saucepan of boiling water.

'Dad,' she heard Kate saying, 'what's wrong?'

'I'll make us all a cup of tea,' said Mrs Skerritt. 'No use trying to sleep in this morning. Why on earth did

Stafford ring so early? Later on would have done just as well. Couldn't wait to pass on a bit of bad news.'

Coming into the kitchen she jumped at the sight of Meredith, then looked at the saucepan on the stove. 'What on earth are you doing?'

'I had a dream,' said Meredith. 'I woke up.'

'Woke needing instant noodles. Couldn't you wait for a proper breakfast?'

'I didn't know everyone else would wake up early, too,' Meredith said, trying to hear what her father and Kate were saying as they exclaimed and shouted in a broken chorus of despair.

Their voices were still bouncing backwards and forwards when she came out into the sitting room, her bowl of noodles against her chest and prepared to listen in.

'Right on, Dad!' Kate was saying, thumping her father on the shoulder. 'He won't know what hit him when we get going. He'll race back overseas. It'll be a lot safer for him in Sydney.'

'It's not really so safe for him these days,' said Meredith's mother. 'Apparently there's a big group, a conglomerate that's moving in on him. "Eyot Undertakings", according to Judith Appleton. Something like that, anyway.'

'Undertakers are people who arrange funerals,' said Rufus. 'Idiot Undertakings!'

'Eyot! It's the name of the man who runs it, Harvey Eyot, and as well as that it's a word for a small island – at least I think it is,' said Mrs Skerritt uncertainly.

Flick!

Meredith quickly looked towards the window.

Outside, the morning light had grown stronger and brighter. That fist of rock rose out of the sea, encircled by an amulet of mottled gold. Above the gorse she could see streaks of scarlet thrift. It suddenly looked as if, there below the fist, crimson were trickling down into a yellow cuff. Kaitangata was bleeding, or perhaps, thought Meredith wildly, the blood that seemed to be trickling from between the rocky knuckles was being squeezed from a lost child, secretly crushed for fifty years by the island's clenching fingers. It was as if her father's angry cries had shocked the island into that other, older life that only she seemed to know about. But then she knew, as no one else did, that Kaitangata was never as restful as it pretended to be. It was always listening in.

10

'You know what?' Rufus said to Meredith, as they walked from the school bus stop down the road that led between their donkey paddock and the Carswell boatshed. 'Allan Ponty says his father's on Marriott Carswell's side.' Rufus spoke quietly for someone who was usually a shouter. He sounded puzzled and a little subdued.

But Meredith was not surprised . . . not by then. You could easily tell what the various families thought about the new District Scheme by listening to what the kids at school had to say. The Pontys, whose orchard was on the western side of the Skerritts' land, and the Shepherds and the Appletons, further along towards the head of the bay, were all excited and hopeful of subdividing their land into house sections, then selling it for a lot more money than they had paid for it in the first place. It was tempting to believe they would become suddenly rich. And both the Shepherds and the Appletons, families who had lived in the bay for longer than the Skerritts, seemed to be saying that they were the *true* people of the bay and had the most right to say what was needed, just as Mr Skerritt felt that he and his family had more right to be there than anyone who might have come after them.

'It's easy for your dad to yak on about the environment,' said Oliver Shepherd. 'He's only got two hectares and a few donkeys. But suppose he could cash in big himself – well, he wouldn't be such a raving greenie then, would he?'

'You've got to be *realistic*,' said Sharon Ponty. Sharon and Meredith spent a lot of time together but they were not altogether best friends, for Sharon was a year older than Meredith, and bossy with it. Suddenly she was laying down the law about the bay and Marriott Carswell's possible plans for it. 'We're too close to the city to escape development – and the land's not all that great for farming anyway. I mean, it's been a real struggle after last year's drought. No let-up!'

'You're just saying that because you've heard grown-ups saying it,' Meredith replied. She knew this was true, because of the way Sharon came out with the word 'realistic'. Anyone could hear the echo of some confident adult voice underlying Sharon's.

'And you're just jealous,' Sharon replied, sounding much more like her usual self this time. Soon after this Allan and Sharon stopped hanging out at the Skerritts' after school.

For a week or two the proposed District Scheme hovered above the Skerritt family, like a dark angel, wings spread, whispering curses. The fringe of grass at the End of the World, the hills before and behind them – all things which had once felt as if they would last for ever – suddenly seemed frail and easily destroyed, though Mr Skerritt certainly tried to protect that old life. There were meetings of other anxious families in the Skerritt sitting room, and the new District Scheme, a block of ring-bound pages with an elegant photograph of the bay on the cover, went from hand to hand. It was studied, photocopied and scrawled on, and had notes, crosses and fierce exclamation marks drawn in its margins. Beside the till in the local store a petition appeared. *We the undersigned* . . . it began, and went on to talk about preserving the unique rural character of the bay communities. Every time they stopped off for milk and cat-food, or anything that Mrs Skerritt had forgotten to buy at the city supermarket, Meredith and Rufus would check who had signed the petition. Their own family name stood boldly at the top – first their father's name and then their mother's. Kate, Meredith and Rufus had not been allowed to sign because they were not ratepayers. Mr Skerritt had pressed his pen so hard on the paper that the ghost of his signature showed up on the pages below, hovering angrily over every other entry. No Ponty names appeared on the petition, and there were no Appletons or Shepherds. 'Only one councillor has signed,' said Mr Skerritt gloomily, which proved that he studied the petition too, when he thought his children were not watching. He began saying, 'People will be sorry . . . but it'll be too late by then.'

Yet within a month the threat had become somehow ordinary – part of everything else, like the season or the weather. Mr Skerritt's first fierce horror was somehow soaked up by meetings, by letters to newspapers, by drafting protests and submissions and talk of a local referendum. As Christmas approached, the gossip about contacting the Department of Conservation and lobbying for the whole bay to be designated as a coastal reserve died away. Plans about holidays and swimming and family get-togethers took over.

11

It was late in the day but still light. Stealing away from family debate, Meredith felt certain that this was a time when Lee Kaa would have finished his gardening and that he too would be stealing time from everyday life, to sit on the log on the foreshore and play his saxophone. Sure enough, she could hear the mellow sound as she came towards the little spike of rock that separated one stretch of the beach from the next. The music seemed to reach out to meet her, to wrap itself around her like a melodious snake that danced her onwards.

'Well, how are things going in the Skerritt world?' Lee asked her. 'Exciting times?'

'Pretty exciting,' said Meredith. 'Mostly Dad and Kate shouting, and Rufus trying to egg them on, and Mum trying to quieten them down.'

'I can imagine,' said Lee.

'It's not that Mum isn't on Dad's side,' Meredith hastened to say. 'She's just somehow more . . . more . . .' She hesitated.

'More resigned,' suggested Lee. Meredith frowned.

'Are *you* resigned?' she asked.

'Ah, there's a question!' Lee replied. 'See, I've fought my own wars . . . won a few, lost a few. I did sign your dad's petition, though. Anyhow, now let's play.' He played a few notes himself before handing the sax over to her. He listened as she began, wavering a little at first, then settling into the sound and the song. The air darkened around them and it almost seemed as if the sound of the saxophone darkened too.

'Now!' said Lee, standing up. 'Off you go or your brother will come dancing along, looking for you.'

Meredith stood up too. The family were used to her wandering off on her own, but it was true that they would come calling for her if it got really dark and she wasn't home.

'Might not see you again until after Christmas,' Lee said. Suddenly he sounded shy. 'Hey! I've got a present for you.' He reached down behind the log and came up with a shoebox holding a huge shell – a great spiral spinning to a point.

'Listen!' said Lee. He put his lips against the pointed end and blew. A curious sound came out of it – not the pure and golden note of the saxophone but a sound that seemed to struggle into the world through sand and moss.

Flick!

Meredith saw Lee's head turn as she found her own head turning, to look across the twilit harbour to Kaitangata, a black shape against the sky.

'No use looking that-a-way,' said Lee. 'Watch this!'

He blew again, holding the shell in his right hand and flapping his left hand over the wide mouth of the shell. The sound rose, then sank away. It came towards her and then retreated.

Lee stopped blowing.

'See what I've done?' he said. 'I've cut the tip off the shell and fitted a little mouthpiece onto it. It's not like the sax . . . but one thing links into another.'

'Flute to sax and sax to shell,' said Meredith. 'Can you play any sort of tune on it?'

'You can get a bit of rhythm out of it,' Lee replied. 'And there's always the sound, coming and going. Yeah! That sound might be enough.' Then, very deliberately, he looked past her. Meredith turned. The beach was empty. 'Plays a sort of lullaby, perhaps,' Lee said. 'It's hard to get some babies to sleep.'

Lee and Meredith stared at one another in the twilight.

'*Do you hear it flicking too?*' she almost asked him, but in the end she just grinned and took the big shell he held out to her.

'Thanks,' she said. 'Big huge thanks, Lee!'

'Happy Christmas,' Lee said. 'And if I see you again before Christmas comes, I'll say it again. Happy Christmas twice over.'

12

The Skerritts enjoyed Christmas that year, once city people stopped asking Mr Skerritt to get their gardens in order for the holidays. Granny and Grandpa Skerritt, who had moved to the warmer north a few years earlier, came south for Christmas.

'It's just so beautiful here,' Granny Skerritt said, over and over again. 'Funny how when you actually live in a place you never look at it properly.'

'Worth fighting for, isn't it?' Mr Skerritt said. 'And believe me – we're going to fight. We'll organise, you'll see.'

'We're going to fight,' said Kate, like her father's echo.

'Why don't you come back and live here again?' Rufus asked his grandmother. 'We'd cut lots of firewood for you so you'd stay warm and we'd come round visiting every day.'

'Hard to resist an offer like that, isn't it?' said Mrs Skerritt, grinning her two-ways grin. 'Rufus loves cutting firewood.'

'Or you could buy more heaters,' said Rufus quickly. 'They don't ruin the forests.'

'They use power, though,' said Kate sternly. 'Rivers get dammed and whole forests are drowned just so that people like you can run heaters.'

The days went scudding past like yachts on windy water, each one the same, each one different, and the submissions against the District Scheme were still not quite finalised. 'Marriott was shrewd, releasing the plan just when he did,' said Mr Skerritt, speaking as if the whole scheme were part of Marriott's private plot. 'People go away on holiday and forget about home problems for a while.'

They picnicked on Kaitangata. Fire restrictions had come in just before Christmas, so there were no island barbecues, but they filled their picnic baskets with long loaves of French bread, salad tenderly folded in clean teatowels, slices of Christmas ham, thermoses of coffee and tea, and bottles of lemonade. Meredith and Rufus and even Kate ran up, down and over Kaitangata as if they were exploring it for the first time. Hundreds of yellow flowers bobbed along the edges of the tracks. Rufus called them dandelions.

'Hawksweed!' Kate corrected him. 'Look! Thin stems, not fat ones! And those blue flowers that look as if they're just hanging in the grass without any stems at all, they're harebells, I think.' The waves offered the sand present after present – streamers of fine red seaweed and the hundreds of shells shaped like the horns of tiny sea-going unicorns, along with the rubbish dropped out of boats or washed away from other people's picnics. When her father organised the family to clean up (exclaiming 'Pollution! Pollution!' in the irritated voice that Rufus copied so well), Meredith tested herself against her memory of dream–terror by deliberately picking up any stranded gloves, fearing as she did so that their plastic fingers would suddenly tighten on hers. But they remained nothing but gloves, swollen only with wet sand. Far stranger were the feelings Meredith had from time to time that somebody else was moving around Kaitangata, watching them from behind rocks and gorse . . . which was quite possible, since other people were free to picnic there. But no one else seemed to feel what Meredith could feel, or see what she believed she could see. She was not sure she was seeing it, either.

Yet what do you do when, in the middle of your holiday cleaning and collecting, you find yourself staring down at a bouquet of formally arranged flowers? – flowers so fresh that they could not possibly have been thrown up by the sea? It was a hot summer day, but Meredith felt herself grow chilly looking at those beautiful flowers. The dark red roses (still opening), the love-in-a-mist, the sprays of what she now knew to be Queen Anne's lace, the paper frill and the white ribbons were immaculate. The scent of freesias seemed to rush up towards her, filling her whole head. Meredith shut her eyes, and breathed out, refusing to accept any presents Kaitangata might offer her. Shivering, she turned and walked blindly away. A few metres off, pretending to be picking up one of the many pieces of water-washed glass that lay like jewels among the shells, she bent over and secretly looked back under her own arm. The patch of sand where the flowers had waited for her was empty. 'You're dreaming,' she told herself severely. 'Dreaming while you're awake ... if you *are* awake, that is.' But if you were having a waking dream, would it be the sort of dream you could ever wake out of? Could you wake when you were awake already, or would you *have* to go on dreaming it for the rest of your life?

At New Year they went to a party at the Kaa Inlet.

'Let's all dance,' said Mrs Skerritt. 'I could really use some light-heartedness.'

'Amen to that!' exclaimed Mr Skerritt, giving her a bear hug and waltzing her away.

'So! How's it going?' said a voice. Meredith turned to find Lee Kaa grinning down at her. 'How about a dance? You do your thing, and I'll just stand here swaying. That way I won't get too dizzy.'

'OK!' said Meredith, grinning back. They faced each other, smiling and dancing in their different ways.

'You keeping in mind what I told you, back a bit?' asked Lee, swaying slowly. 'Steering clear of Kaitangata?'

'We've had a few picnics there,' Meredith admitted. She looked up at Lee. 'Do you ever dream about it?'

'Sometimes,' said Lee.

'Do you ever *hear* it?'

'I used to,' he said rather sadly. 'Back when I was a bit younger than you. But then Shelly disappeared and after that – silence. Silence for about fifty years.'

'*I* hear it,' said Meredith. 'I hear it calling for something to *eat*. I think it's hungry. And I think Marriott Carswell might have something to do with it waking up. I mean, my granny was remembering things the other day, and she was telling us the Gentrys were planning to build a house on Kaitangata before Shelly disappeared out there, and now Marriott Carswell's planning to change the whole bay.'

Lee swayed and nodded.

'First there was me, and now there's you,' he said.

'Maybe when that little old island wakes it needs someone to talk to.'

'I see a bit every now and then,' Meredith admitted. 'But mainly I *hear*. *Flick!* Someone calling in. A sound, but not really a sound.'

'They say it's a Maori thing,' said Lee. 'But Pakeha, Maori, I don't think it matters too much. I remember Shelly was set at a bit of an angle to the rest of her family. She was a wanderer, and girls were expected to stick around home back then.'

'Did she have that very fair hair?' asked Meredith, remembering the child–figure she had seen on the island. 'Young-whitish, not old?'

'She did!' Lee almost snapped it out, but looking as if he were asking her a question, not answering the one she had asked him. The music stopped and people clapped. Lee went on. 'She went out to Kaitangata for that birthday picnic and never came home again. So the island might borrow her shape from time to time. I mean, *she's* not using it any more . . .' His eyes seemed to bore into her, and his voice sank into a whisper. 'We are what we *eat*. 'Nuff said, eh?'

And then, as they stared at each other, a cry went up that it was two minutes to midnight, and everyone had to sing *Auld Lang Syne*, and *Po kare kare ana*, the one song in Maori that everyone, even the non-Maori speakers, knew by heart.

So Meredith began the New Year thinking, as she sailed and picnicked, hugging her grandparents, arguing with Rufus and living an ordinary–extraordinary family life, of what Lee Kaa had told her as they danced. She had the idea he might have told her even more, if midnight and the New Year hadn't interrupted him.

13

Suddenly, the holidays were over. Granny and Grandpa Skerritt said goodbye in a way that was both sad and smiling. Mr Skerritt went back to work, loading his small truck with gardening tools and setting off to trim and dig. Sometimes Mrs Skerritt went with him, for she could work a chainsaw, hammer a nail and turn a compost heap with the best of them. The oldest donkey foal was sold, and went off to a new home. And soon it would be time for school again. Kate would be catching the big bus that carried students over the hill to the college, while Meredith and Rufus would take the minibus to their smaller school, a couple of miles down the road in the opposite direction. The house lost its untidy, sling-anything-anywhere, holiday feeling as Mrs Skerritt began a brisk New Year tidying – 'spring-cleaning', she called it, even though it was late summer.

'Put this stuff away,' she ordered. 'Shove the photo albums at the end of the bottom bookcase shelf, Meredith. I think there's room if you squeeze a bit.'

Meredith managed to push the photograph albums in beside a series of Life books about famous painters. Then she went on sorting through the carton which had been dumped on the window seat, so that Mrs Skerritt (who had begun at ground level with mopping) could vacuum effortlessly. A green triangle with a gold centre looked out from under the ancient folds of newspaper, lining the carton. A dusty book, bound in green and gold, had been trapped there, probably for years. As Meredith pulled it out, a small, square blue box slid out along with it.

Meredith opened the box. It was lined with dark blue velvet and held a silver ring, embossed with long, entwining fingers . . . two hands meeting and clasping one another. She slid it onto her own finger and held out her hand at arm's length, wondering where she had seen that ring before. Overhead, the vacuum cleaner fell silent, and Meredith remembered. It was Rufus who had described a ring like this one. She remembered who had been wearing it, too.

'Hey Mum,' Meredith called up the stairs. 'Guess what? Marriott Carswell wears a ring like this one.' Her voice sounded odd in her own ears, disapproving, but also a little frightened.

'What?' exclaimed Mrs Skerritt. 'What ring?' She came charging downstairs, and Meredith held out her hand, fingers spread. An odd, half-smiling expression flitted across her mother's face. Meredith could not believe it. Her mother suddenly had a *flirting* look. As she pulled the ring off Meredith's finger, she dropped it, and it tinkled on the floor, making a soft yet metallic wheeling sound as it rolled away. Meredith ran after it and snatched it up before it disappeared under the piano.

'Well,' said Mrs Skerritt. 'You've discovered something that's almost a guilty secret. Did you say Marriott is still wearing his?' Mrs Skerritt shook her head. 'Poor old Marriott!'

'Was Marriott Carswell your *boyfriend*?' asked Meredith, astounded to think her mother might ever have loved anyone except her father.

'Oh, we went out together, years ago,' Mrs Skerritt said. 'Before your father came back to the bay.'

'Does Dad know?' asked Meredith.

Mrs Skerritt gave her an impatient look.

'Of course he does,' she said. 'There was nothing much to it. Nothing *heavy*, though your father loves to think he *saved* me.' Then she stopped, and seemed to think twice about what she was saying. 'Well, it wasn't serious as far as *I* was concerned anyway. Marriott acted all devastated for about five minutes, but that's the sort of guy he was . . . is. I mean he's one of those people who just must *win*, no matter what. He was really nasty about it back then . . . told a lot of lies about me, which really hurt at the time. That's partly why your dad is so savage about him. And, even now, Marriott probably loves the thought of getting his own back, just because I slung him over all those years ago.'

'What sort of lies did he tell about you?' asked Meredith.

'Lies about what we'd done together . . . that sort of thing,' said Mrs Skerritt rather vaguely. 'But then within a week or two he was going out with Sally Appleton and whizz-bang! they were married well before me and your dad. So, don't let that old stuff worry you! It's ancient history.'

'But he gave you a *ring*!' exclaimed Meredith. 'And he's still wearing one just like it.'

'OK – maybe he was more serious than I was,' said Mrs Skerritt, shrugging. 'Or perhaps he just happens to like that particular ring. Mind you, I – well, looking back I suppose I led him on a bit. But it was such fun having a boyfriend with a lot of money. And I didn't dream for a minute that your father would come back from overseas. He won that scholarship and whoosh! he was off and away, swearing we'd never see him again. I mean, I'd always had a bit of a crush on your father. A lot of girls did, because he was *so* neat.'

'Neat?' exclaimed Meredith, thinking of her father's straggling ways.

'Not *neat* – neat!' said Mrs Skerritt. '"Neat" meaning, you know, *spunky*. Wild hair ... a dancing step. A bit like Rufus, really. Funny to think of it now, but your dad couldn't *stand* the bay in those days.' She sat down on the window seat, held the ring up and looked at Meredith through it. 'I really thought he'd gone for ever. Just think! If he hadn't come back when he did, your name might have been Meredith Carswell.'

'Don't!' cried Meredith, hating the thought of being anyone except herself. Her mother reached out and hugged her.

'I was only joking,' she said. 'Joking with myself, really. Merry, I *love* our donkeys and our little truck and our gardening greenie life. Marriott *is* a bit of a monster – always was. He can be really, *really* spiteful. But I think he's a bit lost too – always was and always will be.'

'He'd never be as *neat* as Dad,' declared Meredith.

'No way!' agreed Mrs Skerritt. 'But back when we were all at school together, I must say your dad and one or two others did give Marriott a hard time something which your father hates to remember now. Marriott began it all – well, mostly he began it; he was always a bit of a skite. But there were times when they gave him more than he ever bargained for. And back then he was – what do they say these days? – vertically challenged.'

'Vertically challenged?' repeated Meredith, screwing up her face.

'Shortish,' said her mother, holding her hand at knee height. 'Of course, he's every bit as tall as he needs to be these days. Being rich adds to your height, doesn't it? And now it's our turn to be challenged – *financially* challenged.' She laughed.

'He's a rich ratbag,' Meredith said quickly, still haunted by that other family of children her mother might have had. She imagined a ghost of herself, same hair, same eyes, but with Marriott Carswell's lopsided grin. She imagined other versions of Kate and Rufus along with children who had never been born. For a moment they hovered in her head like ghosts, shut out of life because Kate and Rufus and Meredith herself had crowded in ahead of them. 'Has he actually got any kids?' she asked, a little surprised (seeing there had been so much gossip about Marriott Carswell) to find she did not know.

'Two by his first marriage to Sally,' said Mrs Skerritt. 'They're up in Auckland, I think. One by the second – but I never knew his second wife. Neither of his marriages lasted. And if I'd married him it wouldn't have lasted either. He'll never be half the man your father is. But how do you know he still wears a silver ring like this one?'

Meredith reminded her mother that she and Rufus and Kate had met Marriott Carswell out on Kaitangata before Christmas.

'No wonder he kept staring at Kate,' Meredith said. 'He told Kate she looked just like you. And kept looking up and down her legs.'

'Oh did he indeed?' said Mrs Skerritt, sounding suddenly annoyed. 'Well, his luck's out again. Kate might *look* a bit like me, but she's your dad's girl through and through. She wouldn't give anyone like Marriott the time of day.'

'She hates him,' Meredith agreed, staring down at the ring and at the two hands folded so calmly and confidently together.

'That ring always reminded me of the sort of ornament they used to put on graves back in the old days,' said Mrs Skerritt. 'I used to imagine it tightening around my finger . . . cutting off the circulation or something. Oh well! Back to the slaughterhouse.' At the bottom of the stairs she glanced back over her shoulder 'And hey, Merry, better not mention that ring to your father. He can get a bit jealous at times, because Marriott's done so well. In a secret, fairytale way Dad wouldn't mind being rich, but of course he'd want to be rich for noble ecological reasons.'

She winked at Meredith, and disappeared. A moment later the vacuum cleaner started roaring again.

Meredith put the ring on again. It was too big for her, yet she rather enjoyed the heavy, grand feeling of a silver ring. Stretching her hand out in front of her, admiring the look of it, she suddenly remembered the enchantress she sometimes became in her dreams. Looking along her own outstretched arm as if she were sighting something along the barrel of a gun, she put on her magical *calling* voice. 'Shelly! Shelly Gentry!' she whispered. The words seemed to run across the skin of her arm like drops of water. *Flick!* It seemed someone was trying to answer the call. Meredith was suddenly frightened at what she was doing. Quickly she slid the ring off, pushed it back into the blue box, dropped the box into the carton, and picked up the green-covered book instead.

Once she was holding it, she remembered that someone had once shown it to her. It was an old history of the bay written on behalf of a group called the League of Mothers. As she flicked through the pages, she glimpsed recipes, anecdotes, recollections, pieces of family history. Some pieces were autographed. There were names of the Kaa family, the Appletons, a Mrs Jeffrey Carswell, a Daphne Ponty. A flower, dried and dusty, had dropped from between its pages. *Flick!* A picture blinked at her from one of the pages, and was lost. Meredith forced herself to turn back slowly, then found herself staring at an old photograph with a sad black frame around it.

The girl in the photograph, rather younger than she was, smiled back at her, as if they were old friends . . . a girl with fairish hair which looked as if someone had taken a lot of trouble to make it curl. But it was not her arranged curls or the frilly dress, or the birthday cake standing on the table beside her, that made Meredith catch her breath. It was the bunch of flowers she was holding – red roses, love-in-a-mist and Queen Anne's lace caught up in a paper frill and tied with white ribbons.

'Shelly Gentry,' said the name under the picture. The small print seemed to come alive, writhing under Meredith's gaze. 'Shelly Gentry on her tenth birthday.'

'Kaitangata twitch!' Meredith said aloud, as if she were speaking a spell. 'Kaitangata witch!'

'What did you say?' called her mother from somewhere above her.

'Nothing!' Meredith shouted back, wondering if her mother could hear the crackle of fear in her voice.

Then Rufus leaped into the room, struck a graceful pose, saw her expression and changed to a stage gesture of alarm.

'What's wrong?' he cried, leaning away from her as if she had something catching.

'Nothing!' repeated Meredith, and made herself look down at the picture one last time. Then she shut the little book as tightly as she could, holding it closed between her palms. The cover seemed to twist horribly against her skin as if the child she had just imprisoned was trying to force her way out from between the pages. Meredith threw the book back into the box.

She watched it narrowly, but its cover didn't flip open, nor did its pages flutter, for after all, it was just a book, and the photograph was just a photograph of someone long gone – a girl called Shelly Gentry, who fifty years ago had vanished during a birthday picnic on Kaitangata. Meredith did not turn to look back through the window at the island out there, but somehow found the shape of it forming *inside* her eyes. And she found herself longing to set off in the blue canoe, even though some other part of her mind fluttered like a lost spirit-moth, crying, 'Stay away! Stay away!'

*'I've just come back from a cannibal isle
Called Ti-tiddly-i-ti Isle . . .'*

sang Rufus, dancing again.

'What are you singing that for?' asked Meredith, and was surprised to hear how angry she sounded. Rufus was surprised too. He stopped his dancing.

'It just came into my head,' he said in an injured way. 'The door was open and it walked into me.'

'Ha ha!' was all Meredith could say. After all, uninvited guests were always crowding into her own head, banging into each other, arguing and abusing. There was no good reason to feel cross with Rufus, simply because he was singing an old song which she had enjoyed herself for many years. So she grinned and shrugged and went on with the rest of the day, reading, then watching television, then having dinner, doing homework and being read to, along with the rest of her family, by her father before going to bed, and at last, to sleep.

14

Meredith pushed the blue canoe into the sea, scrambled into it and began paddling towards the island through that curious metallic light, which somehow darkened around her as the sea deepened under her. Where had she seen that glow – that exact glow – before? But of course she was being silly. Light could never be *exactly* the same as itself. She must be remembering wrongly. *What time of day is it?* she wondered. *Is it morning? Where's the sun?* Her mother's donkeys lined up along the fence above the house and shouted down, asking their usual question, then answering it in the same breath. *Hee? Haw! Hee? Haw!* Once again Meredith felt certain she had heard that exact sound before – it was as if the donkeys had managed to tape their voices and were now replaying the same cry. *Hee? Haw! Hee? Haw!* they were still asking and answering as the canoe scraped up onto

Shelly Beach. The western end of the island was blanketed by fog, but the sharp eastern end was bright with sunlight – or something like sunshine. It certainly shone.

So Meredith made for that bright shore, going from one little beach to another, and scrambling up and over the fingers of rock that thrust out into the sea, then wound her way over sand and broken shells, following a tideline of sticks and wet pine cones – of other things too. With increasing uneasiness she passed first the skeleton of a fish, then a yellow glove and then, within another two steps, found herself staring down at a sodden black sandal, seized by something close to terror – for she had known exactly what it was she was going to see, half a second before she actually saw it.

But she could not turn back ... not this time. She must go on. So on she went until she reached the eastern end of Kaitangata where she forced herself to pause and stare out to the mouth of the bay, pretending that she had come to stand at the pointed end of the island like a captain of old standing in the bow of his ship, watching the weather with narrowed eyes. All the time she knew she would have to turn, and look along the northern beaches.

Hee? Haw! Hee? Haw! cried the donkey voices.

She turned, and the light immediately seemed to alter around her, to grow harder and more brassy, while the sky, though it remained blue and cloudless, seemed to settle over her as if she were an egg of possibility that needed brooding. And now Meredith saw what she had already known she would see. The linked beaches along the northern side of Kaitangata were smooth and empty of any human trace except for the signs. HAND BEACH said the first one in white printing on blue. Meredith looked on past this sign to the one on the next headland, while on the third . . .

'No way!' said Meredith aloud and tried to turn back on her own tracks, only to find that thick mist had come up silently behind her. Though the northern beaches were flooded with sunlight, those on the south must now be blotted out. Meredith understood that the world was rolling itself up after her. She could not bear to walk into that mist, groping her way blindly back towards her blue canoe. For, if she put out an uncertain hand, what old bouquet of flowers might be slipped into it – what silver fingers might entwine with hers, drawing her forward into a chilly embrace.

There was nothing to do but to walk on, keeping just ahead of the fog which crept silently at her heels, like a well-trained dog. In the distance, on the third headland, dark shapes were waiting for her, one standing a little in front of the others, and Meredith wondered if Shelly

Gentry could possibly be both in front of her and behind her at the same time.

Then, suddenly, her dream muscles remembered something her brain had forgotten, and she found herself leaping sideways, and just in time. The raw pink fingers straining up through the sand to snatch at her ankle clamped shut on air. In leaping aside she found she had put herself within reach of a blue glove, which also snatched at her, and she leaped again, sweat forming on her forehead, for now the sand in front of her rippled as if the Kaitangata twitch was alive in it. It rippled; it blistered. The blisters swelled and burst, blossoming into other snatching hands, some of them brown and lean, some of them brightly-coloured, smooth and nail-less, but all writhing with a horrid, urgent, *island* life of their own. Among the large hands, all straining avid fingers, she saw a small pale hand, not snatching but simply opening and closing in the Kaitangata air. Something about the very meekness of this small pale hand, its transparent fingernails and soft palm, frightened Meredith more than any of the other horrors.

Though they could obviously feel her footsteps, though they swivelled on hidden wrists, the hands were working blindly. Gasping and dancing, Meredith skipped between them, and found herself safe at last on the rocks that thrust out between Hand Beach and the beach beyond it. EYE BEACH said the next sign.

Meredith jumped across the long rockpools, and collapsed onto the sand beyond. A soft rhythm came out of the mist that had collected behind her as if the hands had begun simultaneously to snap their fingers.

Eye Beach ran from the edge of the sea back to a high bank – almost a little cliff. It would take Meredith about half an hour to walk around the whole island and reach her blue canoe. Still, half an hour was not so very long, not now the worst was over – and her first few steps were almost light-hearted. Then suddenly she felt an all-over prickling, and knew that it was *not* over. Something was watching her . . . and the gaze she felt falling on her was not a human gaze.

Meredith stopped again. A small wave, scarcely more than a ripple, dark with suspended sand, flopped onto the shore, making an insignificant *wet* sigh, before running back towards the sea. Meredith could hear the tiny, prickling sound of that water soaking into the sand. The watchful island silence took over once more; another wave lifted and flopped over. And, then, as this wave swept back in turn, Meredith became aware of another sound – a fine, *sifting* sound – coming from the small cliff to her left. Grains of fine soil were falling from under its green fringe onto the shore below. Below the fringe, someone had cut a long oval into the hard, dried earth of the bank. And once Meredith had seen it (as if it needed her to witness what it was planning to do), the oval quivered within its own outline, and the soil fell faster.

Then the cliff opened a great eye and *looked* at her.

The eye had no white to it. Its iris was dark and glittering with grains of embedded quartz, but its pupil was a black space, greedily sucking light from the surfaces of sea and sand, so that as light fell *into* it, an accelerating twilight seemed to surge around her . . . a twilight with force, like wind or tide, a twilight which spun Meredith around, and swept her towards the eye. The pupil now became a pit into which everything must fall – and somehow she was no longer looking *up* towards it, but *down* into it. Meredith let out a cry. Too late! She was already falling into that circle of nothing, and somewhere behind her the eye was closing its lid. Darkness rushed into her open mouth, down her throat, into her lungs and stomach, up though her nose and into her brain.

She was throttling on darkness, dying there under the surface of Kaitangata. She was becoming part of its inner night.

And then she woke up. At least it was a sort of waking, though what was around her was certainly not the room in which she had gone to sleep. Meredith found herself hanging in a huge space, burning with grains of quartz, all set in patterns she recognised. She was smelling a smell she liked, though it was wrong to be smelling it at the moment of waking, and for some reason she thought she must have wet her bed. As she gasped, struggling to work out just where she was, something breathed harshly in her ear. Something tightened around her.

'Merry!' said a voice. 'It's all right. You're safe. It's one of those old dreams of yours . . . dreams . . . dreams. Nothing but!'

Meredith was not lying in her bed. She was on her knees in the sea in front of the boatshed. The glitter above her came from familiar stars. On her right floated the blue canoe, and on her left, her father was kneeling – kneeling in the shallow sea, holding her close, and saying the word 'dreams' over and over again.

15

'Dreams, dreams, dreams!' Mr Skerritt was repeating gently, hugging and holding her. 'You've been walking in your sleep again, Merry. You haven't done that for years.'

'Am I awake now? Really awake?' Meredith cried, collapsing against his shoulder and shivering violently. She was so cold it was like being in pain, and she thought, as she leaned against her father, that she might freeze herself right into him. For how could she ever believe in the beach . . . her father . . . even the cold, which could probably be dreamed like anything else – how could she ever believe in anything ever again? Only a moment ago she had been a mere grain spinning in Kaitangata's eye. And now that dangerous glitter had retreated. It had become nothing more than the distant twinkle of winter stars. No. This must be true. Scorpio, the constellation of autumn and winter, was sprawling above her, curving across the world, and her father was holding her tightly. She was safe.

But for how long? The dream was nothing but a dream, and yet it had drawn her down to the shore, and there was nothing safe about being here in her pyjamas, wet sand working itself between her toes and the canoe nudging her leg with its pointed snout. If she could find her way down the Zigzag without waking up, she could just as easily have paddled all the way over to Kaitangata and walked around its pointed tip to Eye Beach.

'Come on,' said her father gently. 'We're both freezing. Let's get you home, safe and warm.' He bent to pick her up. But then, in spite of everything, Meredith suddenly felt in charge of herself.

'No,' she said. 'It's OK. I can walk.'

So they walked, side by side and hand in hand, back towards the Zigzag. Faint starlight reflected from the water, and Meredith found that now she was used to the dark there was enough light to show her the way. If she closed her eyes, though, a picture of the beach and the bay, much clearer than anything she could see with eyes open, formed behind her lids. No wonder she had been able to find her way in her sleep. The beach and the track that led to it were like a bright map deep inside her head.

'So! What's brought all this on?' her father asked, patting her shoulder.

'I dreamed about the island,' Meredith mumbled between chattering teeth.

There was a short silence.

'My fault,' sighed Mr Skerritt at last, 'raving on about this place the way I do. Sorry! Sorry! Sorry!'

By now, they were nearly at the Zigzag. Looking up Meredith saw the shapes of trees, billowing out against the night sky, which had a transparent blackness all its own. She and her father began to climb. 'I have island dreams myself, these days,' said Mr Skerritt, sounding as if he were talking to himself rather than to her. 'I dream that I get up in the morning, go out into the kitchen to make a pot of tea, glance out of the window – and it's gone . . . all gone, the island, the bay, everything. It's as if it's part of myself that's gone. My whole childhood. Of course there was more to my childhood than the holidays, but somehow it seems as if so much of me was concentrated into being here, and seeing the same beaches . . . the same headlands. And of course the island.' Mr Skerritt was not just staring into space. Meredith could tell he was staring into himself by staring back into past Christmases. 'All gone! Destroyed! But of course it *isn't* really gone,' he added quickly. 'We can still save it.' His voice, which had grown harsher at the thought of the vanishing island, softened with hope. 'Save it for *your* kids, eh?'

'How *can* we save it?' Meredith asked, shivering with cold and with her Kaitangata memories too.

'We *must* save it,' her father said. 'I know I overdo things, at times, but I want to be sure of *something* in a slippery old life.' Ferns brushed against them as they counted six steps this way, then six steps that, climbing steadily towards home.

As they came round the last bend of the Zigzag, he began to talk almost as if he were reminding himself of an old story.

'I couldn't wait to get away from all this when I was a boy,' he said, sweeping his arm sideways in a vague semi-circle. 'I was just like Rufus – thought the best things were happening somewhere else. Anyhow, I won that scholarship and set out travelling.' They reached the top of the Zigzag, and saw a yellow glow spilling through the open back door and the grass glittering with stars of its own. Up the steps they came, being careful on that third rickety step – the one her father was always going to mend next weekend – then crossed the verandah. He shut the door firmly behind them. Meredith knew she must be standing on the hall matting, but she could not feel it properly.

'Hot chocolate?' she suggested quickly, begging and telling in the same two words.

'You need warm, dry clothes more than chocolate,' said her father. 'Cuddle up beside the pot-belly. It's still warm.' But Meredith was already dragging a stool to the wood stove that stood in a corner of the kitchen. She sat, dabbing her feet against it, one at a time, and felt as if she were still dancing.

'How long was I down there?' she asked, wondering if she could have paddled over to Kaitangata and then back again.

'I was right behind you,' her father said. 'But you were a lot quicker than I was. I was really surprised at just how speedy you were out there in the dark.'

I had to go. I was called, Meredith wanted to say, and then made up her mind to keep that idea to herself too.

'There are clean pyjamas on the hot-water cylinder I think,' her father said. While he collected milk from the fridge and cocoa from the pantry, Meredith changed into the warm, dry nightclothes. The hands of the clock on the mantelpiece were both pointing to twelve.

'Was it fun, being overseas?' she asked, beginning to enjoy the chance to be alone with her father, gossiping at midnight.

'I did that Arts degree in the UK,' her father's voice drifted around the pantry, 'and then I decided to hitch around the world.' Once again he was talking to himself as much as he was talking to her. 'Worked here and there, always taking off when I'd saved enough. I just loved it at first. Working and walking in great cities where famous people had lived. But then – oh, well, I was ill for a while . . . and I couldn't get a real job. I don't know quite what would have happened to me, but Dad sent me my ticket home. And the weird thing – the *really* weird thing was that somehow everything I wanted was waiting for me at home all the time, right here in the bay. It was just so beautiful – the bay I mean. Not beautiful like that touristy picture on the District Plan, but beautiful in some *other* way . . . a secret way, just as if it were being beautiful especially for me. And I met your mother again. Met her *properly*, I mean. Of course we'd known each other at school, but she'd been a couple of classes behind me, which was like being on two different planets in those days. Anyhow, we got married, and she worked while I studied for another degree – horticulture, this time. More my thing, really. And then we bought this bit of land, set up gardening and landscaping – and the donkey stud, too; had you kids . . . everything was all so perfect. And the bay just . . . I don't know – it just *was*.

The hills behind. The sea in front. And Kaitangata.' He fell silent. 'And Kaitangata,' he repeated, rather more briskly as if the name were something he was using to fix the whole bay in his mind.

He passed the cup of hot chocolate to Meredith, who took it eagerly.

'After the meeting tonight, I was a bit wound up. I couldn't just go to sleep,' he went on, 'so I stayed up to do a bit of reading. And then I went for a walk. That was how I came to see you, thank goodness.'

The book he had been reading was on the table. Meredith twisted her head sideways to read the title: *Place Names of the Greater Bay Area*.

'Does it mention Kaitangata in there?' she asked, picking up the book and turning the pages curiously.

Her father paused.

'Well, yes,' he said, sounding rather reluctant for some reason. '*Kai* is the Maori word for food, of course, and *tangata* means people.'

'Food–people! People–food!' said Meredith aloud. 'Oh yes. Lee said the Ngai Tahu had killed people there – and eaten them.'

Just for a moment she had a picture in her head of blood soaking into the sand . . . soaking into the sand . . . and the island somehow lapping it up.

'Lee's a storyteller, not a historian,' said Mr Skerritt dismissively. 'I suppose they may have, a long, long time ago. Or it might refer to a single incident. He doesn't know the difference.'

'Everything gets hungry,' said Meredith (*Flick!* '*Feed!*' demanded something in her head) 'and nothing that gets eaten wants to be eaten.' A lot of old stories ran, fast-forward, through her head – 'The Three Billy Goats Gruff', 'The Three Little Pigs' and 'The Wolf and the Seven Little Kids'. The excitement of nursery tales was all about who managed to eat who. 'Chickens, lambs, fish, none of them want to be eaten.'

'How true,' her father said, smiling at her, but still sounding as if he felt uneasy – far more uneasy than Meredith herself was feeling. 'And with that gruesome thought – what about bed? I'll sit with you if you like . . . sing a song or two the way I used to do when you were little.'

*'I've just come back from a cannibal isle,
Called Hi-tiddly-hi-ti Isle,'*

Meredith sang, teasing him a little.

'Not that song!' he said sternly. 'I don't want you having any more nightmares.' But Meredith knew she was dreamed out.

'Brush your teeth after that chocolate,' he reminded her like a good father. Meredith brushed her teeth like a good girl.

Bending over the handbasin, sniffing the healthy, homely toothpaste smell, feeling the toothbrush push her cheek out sideways as she brushed her back teeth, she let her recent nightmare seep cautiously back into her memory, testing it, in the same way that she sometimes gingerly pressed bruises and scratches, working out how much they might hurt. The snatching hands and the eye of the island still seemed frightening, yet here in the world of warm pyjamas and peppermint toothpaste they also seemed silly. How could something be both ridiculous and terrifying?

Yet dreams could! If, for example, she suddenly found herself waking yet again – if she found that brushing her teeth was part of yet another dream, then her toothbrush, which at this moment seemed such an ordinary, sensible thing, might suddenly seem as mad as a false nose.

Two mornings later, school began again. When the Skerritts went up to catch their different buses at the bus stop, they found bulldozers there before them. A new road was being scraped into the hillside behind their house, and someone had erected a huge sign, covered with words and even a few pictures, right beside the bus stop.

WITTWOOD VILLAGE Exclusive Residential Development. Sections 1000 m² to 4068 m². TOP LOCATION PANORAMIC VIEWS. Swimming, boating, water-skiing, fishing, bush-walks are at your doorstep. Thirty minutes scenic drive to the city. For further information, contact Marriott Carswell Enterprises Ltd or Carswell Realty Ltd Sole Agents.

Above the name *WITTWOOD* was a big picture of the bay, taken from the air, with Kaitangata like a tear low on its cheek. At the bottom of the notice was a little head-and-shoulders picture of Marriott Carswell, wearing a collar and tie so that he looked businesslike and reliable. His lopsided smile mocked the people of the bay, and, perhaps the Skerritts in particular, for now he was looking over their fence and down into their back yard – almost, thought Meredith, as if he were prying into their very lives, laughing to himself as he did so.

PART THREE

16

A few mornings after the Wittwood sign went up and Marriott Carswell's image began peering down between the trees and through their front windows, Meredith's ears opened to the day before her eyes did. Exclamations and the sound of things being put down more forcibly than usual crowded in on her. Once again family voices were being raised. Her parents seemed to be shouting at one another. 'How can it possibly be my fault?' her father was exclaiming.

There was a dragging, struggling sound. Someone was forcing Meredith's door open, pushing her blue chair backwards as they did so. And then her bed began shaking. *The Kaitangata twitch*, thought Meredith, opening her eyes wide and springing upright from her pillows. But the earthquake was Rufus, dancing as he rattled the foot of her bed.

'*Kate's cut her hair.* Really *really short!*' he shouted. 'She's *shaved* her head. Come and see. Now! Come now.' Rufus sounded as if he were terrified that Kate's hair might suddenly grow before Meredith had a chance to see her without it.

It was true. Kate had become a stranger overnight. She sat in her usual place at the breakfast table, staring stubbornly at the plate in front of her. All that was left of the long, thick, shining hair was an uneven, reddish-blonde stubble too short to shine.

'Oh, I can't help it!' Mrs Skerritt was saying. 'I know it was yours, not mine, but I loved your hair the way it was.'

'Mum, I'm a *warrior*,' Kate replied wearily, explaining something that she had obviously explained many times already. 'I'm staunch! And I'm sick of – of certain people organising – always organising and going to meetings and not really doing anything. I want to *do* something.'

'For God's sake,' Mr Skerritt cried, hovering behind her like a useless angel. 'How is shaving your head going to help? And, anyway, you don't have to have short hair to be a warrior. Think of the Vikings! Think of . . .' He stopped, struggling to remember other long-haired warriors. 'Think of your Ngai Tahu ancestors.'

'I'm not them, and I'm not a historic warrior,' Kate declared stubbornly. 'I'm me, Kate, now. At that meeting last week you said we would battle and this is me, battling. Cutting my hair is just the outside sign of it.'

Rufus listened, looking from one to the other with deep appreciation.

'Your fault!' declared their mother, nodding in their father's direction. He took no notice.

'It's like bulldozing native bush. Cutting your hair's just another victory for Marriott Carswell,' he said.

'Not true!' exclaimed Kate. 'I *know* what it means. If you don't – well, too bad about you.'

'Don't speak to me like that,' he exclaimed sharply.

Mrs Skerritt sighed. 'Look, it'll grow again,' she said, trying to comfort her husband. 'Gosh, if Marriott could hear us right now, tearing into each other, he'd laugh his head off.'

Mr Skerritt grew silent. He and Kate still glowered at one another, but there was the beginning of forgiveness in the glowering.

'If you want to make a gesture, that's your privilege,' Mrs Skerritt went on, turning to Kate. 'Just don't talk as if making a gesture was so much cleverer than organising.' Kate looked down at her plate and gave a silly grin.

Rufus couldn't bear to see family drama dying away into nothing.

'She could get tattooed,' he cried, filled with new excitement. 'She could have one of those snakes winding up her arm. Or a skull. Have a skull, Kate. Hey! You could have KILL CARSWELL tattooed across your forehead . . .' (he scraped his thumb across his own forehead to show her just where) '. . . and then everyone who saw you would be able to read—'

'Don't even *think* of it,' Mr Skerritt declared, using a masterful-father voice, but looking stricken, as if he were suddenly terrified that Kate might take Rufus seriously. 'Kate, you don't oppose a slash-and-burn policy by slashing and burning yourself.'

'Maybe I do,' said Kate stubbornly. 'Maybe I become a slash-and-burn *sign*. I'm not the only one. Nick's *shaving* his head.'

'Nick? Nick Chambers?' cried Mr Skerritt, relief creeping into his voice, as he found someone outside the family that he could safely blame. 'Did he put you up to this? I wish you wouldn't get around with him and his lot.'

'It was *my* idea,' shouted Kate, standing up now, and turning to face her father, 'I put *him* up to it. He's got a car, but I'm the one with the ideas.'

'I loved your long hair,' Mr Skerritt said, just as his wife had said a few minutes earlier. He looked mournfully at Kate as she stood up. Pudding, who had been watching closely, barked as if she did not recognise Kate. Pie merely opened his eyes, and then shut them again. Nothing the Skerritt family did could surprise him.

'Well, too bad, Dad,' said Kate in a gentler voice, reaching up to pat first her father's head, and then Pie's woolly one, reassuring both of them. 'Actually, I've wanted to have it short for ages.'

'Hey, Dad, you could shave off *your* hair too,' Rufus now suggested to his father. 'I mean you're a bit bald in the middle already, so you could just . . .'

'Rufus, stop!' said Mrs Skerritt wearily. 'I can't stand much more. OK, Kate's cut her hair and that's that. And now it's nearly bus time. Just get going.'

Kate stood up. She looked across the table. 'Dad, just tell me one thing. What are you actually, ultimately going to *do*?'

Mr Skerritt looked around the table.

'Well . . .' he said, and hesitated.

'Don't say "organise"!' shouted Kate. 'We're past organising. We've got to attack.'

'Attack?' said Mr Skerritt, sounding rather confused this time. 'Yes! Maybe! But after all, Marriott's got the law on his side. No! Let's wait a little . . . wait and see.'

17

And for a while, that's what they did. They waited; they saw.

Huddled in their brightly coloured winter coats and hoods, hugging themselves against the cold, Skerritts, Appletons and Pontys argued at the bus stop, morning after morning, watching curiously as the new road wound its raw way up the hillside.

'Nothing ever stands still,' cried Sharon Ponty. 'We've got to have *progress*.'

'But it's not progress to spoil a place,' Meredith argued with her old friend who was no longer quite a friend, 'and too many people crowding into a place just ruin it. Everyone wants to look at the lovely views, but suddenly the view stops being a view of hills and sea. It turns into a view of other people's houses and television aerials. And then it isn't lovely any more.'

'No one's going to build in front of *you*,' said Sarah Appleton crossly. 'Not unless they build on Kaitangata.'

They all read Marriott Carswell's huge notice over and over again. Even Skerritt donkeys, looking over the back fence, seemed to be reading it too. Rufus quickly learned the words on the notice by heart.

'Panoramic views and *top* location,' he would chant, doing one of his dances around the living room. 'Panoramic views and *top* location!' (making his voice shoot in a high falsetto squawk on the word 'top'). Or he would kneel on the window seat, staring through the wide sitting-room window at Kaitangata and the hills on the other side of the bay, pecking at the view with his crooked forefinger, and intoning, 'Thirty minutes scenic drive to the city – if you have a good car, that is.'

'And only if you drive too fast!' added Meredith.

'Shut up! Shut up!' yelled Kate ferociously. 'Don't encourage him. Mum, they're *joking* about it. It's like laughing at death.'

'Well, there are lots of jokes about death,' Rufus cried back. 'People laugh about it quite a lot.'

Diagrams of projected developments were left in the letterboxes of every ratepayer in the bay, and all opinions, the council said, would be welcomed, but there were so *many* opinions. Meredith thought it was rather like welcoming the three little pigs at the same time as you were welcoming wolves. Farming families from the head of the bay were protesting too, but over an entirely different part of the District Scheme from the part that was upsetting Mr Skerritt, for some of the farmland had been classified as a coastal reserve, which meant farmers would no longer be allowed to put up sheds, or put in new roads, or plant blocks of pine trees without special permission. Mr Skerritt did not object to this part of the plan, for he loved bare hilltops and open slopes, and often grumbled about plantations of pine trees on the foreshore.

'Well, of course we don't want to live hemmed in by pine trees,' he declared grudgingly.

'You're such a pine snob, Carey,' said his wife, trying to tease him into a calm mood again.

'And of course this so-called coastline policy is just thrown in so Marriott can try to make out he's sensitive to conservation issues,' Mr Skerritt went on. 'If he could make a dollar out of that particular land himself, it would be quite a different story.'

'Marriott the Shark!' cried Rufus, sounding a little envious. He held his arms in front of him and mimed a long snapping mouth, 'Marriott Jaws!' His voice changed, 'Hey, did you know that the fish they use in fish and chips is often *shark* meat, and it's *us* eating *them*, not *them* eating *us*? So sharks should be the protected ones.'

'Not sharks like Marriott Carswell,' said Kate.

'Rufus, your father and Kate just *have* to have their villains,' said Mrs Skerritt. 'Now, Carey, you keep calling this District Scheme Marriott's plan. But there are other councillors backing it too, you know. It's a *council* plan.'

'Oh, he's got the whole council in his pocket, no doubt about that,' Mr Skerritt declared, flapping the proposals as if to drive away unseen wasps.

'But who elected the council?' asked Mrs Skerritt slyly. 'A lot of our neighbours *like* the idea of, say, a proper sewerage system at last. Look at that pink section in the middle.'

'Are you saying we need a full-blown sewerage system discharging into the bay?' asked Mr Skerritt, quickly flicking to the pink section of the plan.

'A *fly-blown* sewerage system,' said Rufus, nudging Meredith. 'A *fly*-blown sewerage system! Get it? *Fly*-blown, not *full*-blown! Fly-blown!'

'Of course I get it,' said Meredith impatiently. 'I'm not dumb.'

'Mum, it's *our* bay,' said Kate. She sounded truly distressed. 'Why do you keep sticking up for the plan?'

'Yes, why?' asked Meredith with a meaningful note in her voice that only her mother was meant to hear. Her mother looked at her warningly.

'A full-blown, fly-blown sewerage system . . .' Rufus muttered, stretching his joke out as long as he possibly could.

'I'm *not* sticking up for it. I just want you two to be – I don't know – *prepared*, I suppose. A lot of people – nice, friendly neighbours of ours, people we've known for years, who just happen to have dodgy septic tanks – are going to love the idea of that sewerage system, right? And they might jump at the chance of spreading the cost by taking on a few extra ratepayers – rich ones if possible.'

'Mum, you're such a wimp,' said Kate stubbornly. '*I'm* staunch!' She shook her clenched fist in the air in a way that reminded Meredith of the rocks on the summit of Kaitangata. 'I'm going to fight.'

'Can *I* go to the meeting?' begged Rufus. '*I'll* be staunch, too.'

'No! I know these meetings. They go on for ages,' said Mrs Skerritt. 'They start off all orderly and reasonable with everyone saying that we must work together to find a solution, and they end with friends shouting at each other about democracy, and then never speaking to one another again.'

Meredith knew that this was exactly what Rufus was hoping for.

'We *live* here,' Mr Skerritt said sternly. 'It's our *home*. We have to fight for it.'

'Yes! Fight against orcs like Marriott!' cried Kate. 'If he was in *The Lord of the Rings* he'd be a tool of Mordor.'

Meredith thought she'd been a mere listener for long enough.

'The Pontys *want* to cut their orchard into sections,' she said. 'Sharon Ponty says we need development.'

'So does Allan,' agreed Rufus.

Mr Skerritt looked despairing.

'How can the Pontys bear to spend years and years putting in fruiting trees – beautiful apples and nectarines – and then quite cheerfully smash them with bulldozers?' he asked the sitting-room air.

'Allan reckons his dad won't have to work ever again – well, he won't have to once they've sold off the sections,' cried Rufus. 'And they'll build a new house further up the hill behind us to get a better view. And they'll go to the Gold Coast for the winter and–'

'The only one who'll make big bucks is Marriott Carswell,' said Mr Skerritt, interrupting the list of blessings for which the Pontys were apparently hoping.

'Yes, but couldn't *we* sell a bit, too — just a *little* bit?' Rufus begged. He held up his hand with his thumb and forefinger about a centimetre apart, 'And then get water — not rainwater in tanks, but proper piped water. And then we could build a swimming pool . . .'

'For God's sake, Rufus!' cried his father. 'Why on earth would we need a swimming pool? We've got the whole *bay* at our back door.'

'Yes, but half the time it's low tide,' whined Rufus. 'It's muddy and full of crabs. And if we had a swimming pool . . .'

'Well, we'll *never* have one,' said Mr Skerritt brutally.

'And talking of low tide,' Mrs Skerritt said, 'has Marriott got any plans for Kaitangata? I mean there it is, sitting right in the middle of our best view, and if he . . .'

Flick! Meredith looked around but nobody else gave any sign of hearing that *flick*. The Kaitangata twitch startled everyone, but that *other* Kaitangata twitch — that voice, that Kaitangata heartbeat — was heard by her alone. There it came again! *Flick!* '*You! You!*' *Flick!* '*You! Feed! Feed!*'

'Well, I'm going to tell everyone what *I* think, even if I'm not a ratepayer,' Kate was saying. Her family was only half-listening. They had heard it all before. Only Meredith, who was actually looking at her, noticed Kate's curious expression – defiant yet a little smug too, the expression of someone enjoying a wicked secret.

Rufus laughed.

'A ratpayer!' he cried. 'The true people of the bay – that's us – are full-blown ratepayers, but anyone who agrees with Marriott Carswell is a fly-blown *rat*payer.'

Mrs Skerritt sighed, and began to carry dirty dishes into the kitchen, followed by Mr Skerritt and Kate, still nagging from either side. Rufus jiggled uncertainly for a minute or two, then followed them into the kitchen, while Meredith, glad to be on her own for a few minutes, climbed onto the window seat and looked out through the window.

'There you are,' she muttered, 'Just behave yourself.'

'. . . and after all, if I *really* wanted the bay to stay totally untouched, I wouldn't be living here myself, would I?' said her mother's voice out in the kitchen. 'I'd live in the city, and just enjoy the *idea* of the bay, pure and untouched between bare hills. But we built this house, didn't we? We dug into the slope and levelled the space and poured the concrete foundations. And then we had our kids, and brought in our dogs, and our donkeys and car and our diesel truck. And now we're saying "After us, nobody!" Anyhow, let's get this show on the road. Meredith!' she called, 'Wash-up time!'

The signal came again. *Flick!* '*Feed! Feed!*'

When Meredith went to bed that night she did what she had done ever since her last sleepwalking dream, which was to push her blue chair against the door, and tie one end of her dressing-gown cord to her wrist and the other around one of the bars on the headboard of her narrow bed.

But as it happened, she slept deeply without dreams of any kind.

18

Almost no one put out onto the harbour during the winter. The Trident Cove jet-skis and outboard motors were packed away, and the whole bay fell under a spell of silence. Early-morning light grew somehow reluctant, slinking unwillingly up from behind the hills. Meredith was often the only person out on the water on these late grey afternoons, her hands feeling as if they had been welded by cold to the rhythmically dipping paddle. Out there, in the pearly world of winter, she could imagine herself to be the first and only traveller on a new planet. Gliding around Kaitangata, she pulled on her paddle so slowly that the water barely rippled above the flat surface of the rest of the bay. Kaitangata's warrior fist of rock gestured above her, and if she looked down she saw it again, reflected in the sea, punching downwards now, towards the heart of the world. Sometimes she landed on the island

and walked around it in a state of eerie expectation, studying the wavering ribbons of seaweed debris, that tied the island in on itself. Every shred of plastic, every strand of seaweed, every crushed tin and grain of sand seemed to have as much meaning as the big things of the world – the hills, the daylight moon and the oldest trees. But meaning, whatever it might be, slid away if she tried to give it a name, turning once more into mere flotsam thrown up by the sea.

Of course, there were times when she raced down the Zigzag with Rufus, times when she tore around Kaitangata, scrambling from one beach to another, leaping, without fear across the rocks. Her short brown hair bobbed about her ears, yet in her mind she was transformed into a cloudy, slender creature whose long tresses flowed behind her in streaks of fire. Sometimes she would come to a halt, balancing gingerly on some pitted ridge of volcanic stone, confused at being two different people in one and the same moment. She knew the picture she had of herself inside her head was nothing like the person who looked back at her from the mirror each morning. But who cared! She would shrug, then run and shout again. Both moods, the still one and the running one, were kinds of happiness.

The usual winter storms beat down, but once they

were over the watchful stillness returned. Lee Kaa did not come down to the beach these cold evenings, so there was no chance to practise the saxophone. Up in her bedroom she played the flute, with the door open. Then she would close the door, get the shell from the back of her wardrobe and blow into it softly, filling the room with its strange, mossy note, a sound swelling towards her from some unearthly place. After school Meredith sometimes paddled out beyond Kaitangata, then, laying her paddle across the blue canoe, she would sit looking through her birthday binoculars at the hillside above their house. The bulldozers had retreated, but not before cutting a great, slow, winding reddish word – a word in a language Meredith could not understand – across the hillside.

June was over. Then July. In August the year began to stir and stretch again. The days began to get just a little longer. The puddles by the bus stop stopped icing overnight. Meredith and Rufus and the other minibus children would occasionally see, as they came home from school, groups of people up on the slopes behind the bus stop inspecting sections they might buy and build on.

All through that winter Meredith had continued to set traps for herself – obstacles that would wake her up if she began sleepwalking again. Night after night she would push the blue chair in front of the door, jamming its straight back under the door handle. Night after night she would carefully tie herself to the head of her bed.

'Merry's getting *shy*,' Rufus said one morning at breakfast. 'It's because she's getting – you know!' He sketched two curves in front of his own thin chest. Meredith felt her face grow suddenly hot.

'You shut up!' she cried. 'You don't know anything about anything.'

'Hope *not*!' cried Rufus in a deeply sarcastic voice. 'Hope *not*!' But Kate, walking behind his chair, took hold of his ears, crying 'What are these great jug handles?' and shook his head from side to side, winking at Meredith over his head as she did so.

Their mother looked over at Meredith with a funny *mixed* expression, amused and loving. And was it also, Meredith wondered, a little bit sad? For some reason, her mother's kind glance made her blush all over again.

Yet as Meredith tied her wrist to the head of her bed with the dressing-gown cord (which was long enough to let her turn over in the night, but would bring her up short if she made for the door), she knew that anyone capable of sleepwalking their way down the Zigzag would also be capable of untying the dressing-gown cord and shifting the chair without once waking up.

Sometimes she thought that strange, urgent island voice might echo in her head for the rest of her life, stinging and throbbing every now and then, like a slightly anxious tooth. She might get used to it and just shrug it away. At other times she was sure it was waiting for some weak moment, and then, whether she wanted to or not, she would answer its call.

Little by little, spring began to edge into the bay. Early plum blossom began to show on dark branches. Lambs hurried after their mothers in the paddocks past which the minibus drove on its way to school. Soon it would be Meredith's birthday again. 'You were born when the thrift came into flower,' her mother said, smiling and remembering. Soon the thrift would flower again and she would be thirteen. A teenager . . . something officially different from a child. *Thirteen!* thought Meredith with mixed feelings. Staring at herself in her mirror, she was surprised again at her reflection. There she was, middling tall, middling thin, middling coloured; could that really be her, so definitely *not* an enchantress – not a wild, free creature with a bright mane of flowing hair? She knew all that middling girl's secrets, knew that the middling girl secretly believed herself to be remarkable. But what did anyone else think, seeing that particular face . . . hearing that particular voice? What could anyone think but 'middling'?

She was sure her dreams were not middling dreams. Sometimes she remembered them, and sometimes she simply remembered dreaming. One night she dreamed she was on Kaitangata, climbing up under the gorse exactly as she had climbed almost a year ago. There, right before her, the ground had caved in. She crept towards the edge on hands and knees and looked down into the new underrunner. At first she thought it was full of water and that she was seeing her own reflection, but then she saw that this hole really fell away to the very centre of the world and that, rising up out of it, was a white-headed child offering flowers. Meredith put out her hand to take the bouquet, but then the girl dropped the flowers and twisted her fingers in between Meredith's, so that their hands were linked like hands engraved on a ring, and began tugging her down into the hole. As they struggled, the girl smiled and blinked at Meredith. Then her eyes dissolved into dry sand which ran in bright, trembling threads down her cheeks. Mud and clay gushed out of her mouth, and dribbled down her chin. The grip on Meredith's wrist was so thin and strong that it hurt, like a tightening noose of wire. Waking, Meredith found herself in the passage outside her bedroom door, tugging hard against the dressing-gown cord, which had pulled around her wrist so tightly that the skin of her hand had darkened and her fingers throbbed once they were set free. She was frightened for a single moment, but almost at once she relaxed, feeling pleased with herself. That dressing-gown cord had worked. It had saved her, perhaps, from that unknown beach – the third beach that lay beyond the beaches of Hand and Eye. As nightmares go, this last one was nasty, but only in an ordinary way.

Later that same morning, she and Rufus scrambled up the road away from the sea to the school bus stop. Above them on the hillside rose scarred slopes crossed with bands of tumbled raw clay, and spiked with the stumps of kanaka and wilding pines snapped like sticks. The new roads curled over the rounded slopes like purposeful worms, writhing across the land and eating it into a different shape.

All the other local children were at the bus stop before them, and everyone was looking at Marriott Carswell's huge notice as if it were completely new. No one turned as they came up, both panting a little.

Meredith could easily see that something had happened to change the notice, but she could not immediately work out what it might be.

Hee? Haw! called the donkeys.

WITTWOOD VILLAGE. *Exclusive Residential Development* said the sign. Except it no longer said 'Wittwood' at the top or 'Carswell' at the bottom. Someone with a spray-can had taken the notice by surprise, and had altered both words.

'SHITWOOD VILLAGE! Arse-well Developments,' read Rufus, clearly feeling he could say such things aloud if they had been written down, where everyone could read them anyway. And then at the bottom, crammed into a speech balloon, there were other words crowded and uneven, misty at the edges as if they were fading into the air.

'That's an "I",' said Rufus, joining the other children, bending and squinting at smudgy, cramped words. 'I am – something. I am an Arse-well and a great big . . .'

'You probably *know* what it says,' said Sharon Ponty, turning towards them with unexpected fury. 'Your dad did it, didn't he? Sneaked up here with a spraycan after dark.'

Rufus straightened.

'He's not a *vandal*,' he said, sounding genuinely upset. 'He's an *activist*.'

'Anyhow, there's another notice back by the pub that's been sprayed,' said Cathy Sullivan, who came from the head of the bay. 'It must be someone with a car, getting around after dark.'

'*They've* got a car,' said Sharon. 'The Skerritts have.

Not much of a one, but it goes. Police should examine it for traces of blood – I mean paint.'

Allan Ponty gave Meredith a weak smile, and Meredith understood that Allan was sick of the fighting. In the beginning it had been exciting, but Allan wanted to forget arguments and hang out with Rufus again.

'Don't *smile* at them,' said Sharon, punching Allan's shoulder. Kate was not the only warrior in their part of the bay.

It was low tide in the harbour. Out beyond the tree-tops the mud seemed somehow iced with light. Two grey herons scavenged busily, and beyond them lay Kaitangata, looking perfectly at ease with the changing world. From this angle, Meredith was tempted to think that the island, as bored with all the arguments as Allan Ponty, had yawned and turned its back on them, and then, effortlessly, dropped off to sleep.

19

The damaged notices were replaced. Once again Marriott Carswell's face gazed across the road and into the Skerritt garden, undefiled and smiling with false innocence. But a day or two later, the notices were sprayed again, and with dirtier suggestions.

'Doom strikes!' yelled Rufus, enjoying it all. 'The phantom sprayer is at work! Mum, do you know what it said? It said . . .'

'I know what it said,' snapped Mrs Skerritt. 'I can read. And if I look out of my bedroom window and up the hill, I can read it all over again. Just don't let me hear you repeating the words on that notice.'

'Absolutely not,' said Mr Skerritt, just as sternly. But Meredith heard him saying to her mother out in the kitchen when he thought the children could not hear him. 'I must say Marriott's been asking for it. No wonder he's a bit reluctant to show his face around here.'

'He's over in Sydney,' said Mrs Skerritt. 'Or he was. He might be back now. Some business complication according to Mr Gair. Some takeover bid or other.'

'I wish someone would take him over,' grumbled her husband. 'Take him over and get him out of our lives, so that things could go back to being the way they were.'

'That Eyot Holdings lot apparently,' Mrs Skerritt said. 'Funny! It sounds quite small, doesn't it, but whatever it is, it's been powerful enough to get Marriott's attention.'

Later Meredith woke. And since she was awake now – awake and thirsty – she decided to go downstairs and get a drink of water. The sound of detectives arguing on television crept in under her closed door, so she knew, even before she untied the old dressing-gown cord, even before she shifted the chair under the doorhandle and then padded along the upstairs gallery, that her parents were still up. She looked in on them on her way to the kitchen.

'Hello, dear,' said her mother. 'Are you asleep or awake?'

'Mostly awake,' said Meredith. 'Awake and thirsty.'

She went through into the kitchen, both dogs following her, just in case. She was looking down at the dogs at the exact moment they suddenly lifted their heads and cocked their ears forward. Pie began to bark and ran for the hall. A heavy knock fell on the front door. Pudding took off, barking too.

'More trouble,' Meredith heard Mr Skerritt saying gloomily, as he got to his feet. 'Must be trouble at this time of night.' His voice changed, as he became truly alarmed. 'Kate! If that damned boy has crashed that bomb of his . . .'

'Might be good news,' Mrs Skerritt called after him. 'The law of averages says it has to be good luck sometimes.'

'I read somewhere that you can toss a coin and it will come down heads fifty times running,' Meredith called, turning towards the partly open door.

Mrs Skerritt did not answer.

'Hello, Tom,' Mr Skerritt was saying. 'What can I do you for?' And then he spoke in such a different voice it sounded as if the stranger at the door might have stabbed him.

'Kate!' he exclaimed.

'Oh dear,' said Mrs Skerritt, springing to her feet, and running to the hall door. 'Is she all right?'

'Of course I'm all right!' yelled Kate from somewhere in the hall, sounding particularly grumpy.

Then Meredith heard the voice of a second man, and knew exactly who that second voice belonged to. Pushing the door open a little further, she looked into the sitting room.

The room had filled up. There was Kate, there was Tom Maxwell, the local policeman, and there was Marriott Carswell himself. He stood there as if he owned the room, yet looked around it curiously. His expression seemed grave, but Meredith was not fooled. Marriott Carswell was a happy man. No matter how he might tuck in the corners of his mouth, his eyes were sparkling with wicked joy. There had been some sort of Skerritt disaster and Marriott Carswell was delighted.

'Kate!' said Mrs Skerritt. 'Darling! What's happened?'

'Perhaps we could have a word,' Tom said, looking at Mrs Skerritt doubtfully. 'I mean, it's nothing too serious in one way. Nothing that can't be mended. But—'

'It's just that I've been spraying *his* horrible signs,' said Kate impatiently, jerking her elbow in the direction of Marriott Carswell, rather as if she longed to be hitting him in the ribs with it. 'And he caught me.'

'She wasn't the only one,' said Marriott Carswell.

'There were two of them. I was planning to work late in the boatshed – the way I do – and I caught them at it. Well, I drove on by as if I hadn't picked up anything unusual, but I parked by the Harpers' drive, and got on the phone to Tom. And I followed the kids when they went on to the next sign. If I'd known it was one of your girls, Carey, I swear I'd have just had a quiet word with you first . . .'

He sounded apologetic, but anyone (thought Meredith) could tell he was only acting, playing out the part of a good-hearted but abused neighbour in front of a policeman.

'You got on the phone?' said Mrs Skerritt a little stupidly. 'I didn't know there was a phone box left between the bay and the city.'

'Mum!' cried Kate scornfully. 'He's the sort of man who has a mobile in every pocket.'

'Spraying signs!' said Mr Skerritt in a curiously heavy voice. He stared at Kate. 'You're the one who . . .'

'Come on, Canary,' said Marriott Carswell. Meredith knew that 'Canary' had been her father's nickname at school. 'Don't blame the kid. She's only been doing what you'd like to do. Maybe you even told her to do it.'

Mr Skerritt fired up at once. 'What are you suggesting?' he asked angrily.

'Now hang on,' cried Tom Maxwell. 'Stay calm!'

'Well, she wouldn't be up to anything like that without a bit of private nudging, would she? Canary by nature as well as by name,' said Marriott, using that falsely good-natured voice. Clearly he was reminding Meredith's father of an old playground insult.

Kate turned on him.

'He didn't think of any of it!' she shouted. 'It was all me. Just me and – and someone I'm not going to tell you about.' Meredith knew this unnamed companion must have been Nick Chambers. Kate spun around and faced Mr Skerritt. 'I was being a warrior.'

'Oh God,' said Mr Skerritt. He flopped into a chair.

'But nobody ever *does* anything!' Kate said half-defiantly, half-pleadingly. 'And while you all whine on about the bay changing forever, everything out there is being pulled to bits. Even you, Dad, you *talk*, but that's all.'

'And you really think that spraying posters with abuse counts as *doing* something?' cried Mr Skerritt.

How Rufus would have enjoyed all this, Meredith thought, but not nearly as much as Marriott Carswell was enjoying it. He was listening to her father, his face pulled into sorrowful lines while his eyes sparkled joyously.

'Now then,' said Tom. 'Marriott, you did promise

that if I let you come along with us there'd be no trouble. So let's keep our heads. And Kate, this business of defacing the notices – like I've already told you there are fines, of course. Those notices cost Marriott money, and not only that . . . well, it's not what you'd call nice language, is it? I mean, if you're so keen on keeping the world beautiful, I can't see why you'd go spraying words like that around – where little kids can see them, too.' As he spoke, he reached into his coat pocket, brought out a spraycan and set it on the corner of the table. 'You'd better have this,' he said to Mr Skerritt.

'It's empty anyway,' said Kate.

'I know we don't see eye to eye over this business, Canary, but I just thought I'd call in to tell you in person there are no hard feelings,' said Marriott Carswell quickly. Meredith thought she could feel her father wincing at this false kindness. 'I certainly don't intend to press any charges, even though it has cost me a bit.' Marriott could obviously feel Mr Skerritt wincing too. He smiled. 'I mean, what with all the argument and abuse and so on – well, naturally the kids get caught up in it too. Of course I would appreciate it if you spent a bit more time looking after your kids and a bit less slagging me off.'

Mr Skerritt took such a slow breath that Meredith

thought she could feel it quivering in her own lungs. Ignoring Marriott, Mr Skerritt spoke to Tom.

'It *is* my fault, Tom,' he said. 'As you know – well, everyone knows, it's no secret – I do feel very deeply about all that destruction up there' (he jerked his thumb upwards) 'and of course Katie's taken my views on board in a big way, so it's really a bit of family loyalty gone wrong.'

'It isn't,' cried Kate passionately. She turned on her father, pointing back over her shoulder at Marriott Carswell. 'He's ruining the bay. If he puts up any more bloody notices – OK, I'll spray them again.'

'No you won't, Kate,' said Mr Skerritt quietly. 'Because if you do anything like that again – just once – I'll withdraw all my objections. You'll force me to stop fighting for the cause.'

'Anyhow, she's safe home again,' said Tom Maxwell, looking relieved as if the worst was over and done with. 'I'll be on my way and leave you to work this out with her, Carey. But make sure you *do* work it out.'

Then he nodded to Mrs Skerritt as he turned to go.

'Nice to see you, Michelle! Use your influence, won't you?'

Marriott Carswell looked past Mr Skerritt, and his eyes lingered on Kate. But then he looked at Mrs Skerritt and Meredith felt that, even though this was the first time he had really looked at her, in a way he had been thinking about her from the moment he first stepped into the sitting room.

'Pretty girl,' he said. 'Takes after you, Mickey. Really sexy legs – nice and smooth, just like yours. I suppose that's why I feel I know her really well. Funny, isn't it?'

'Hang on a minute–' began Tom urgently.

He was too late. Mr Skerritt flung himself forward. Mrs Skerritt shouted 'No, Carey!' as he fell upon Marriott Carswell, bowling him over sideways so that Marriott's face scraped against the door frame, still grinning as it grazed downwards against the wood. Then they both tumbled over and over, wrestling in what looked like a curiously clumsy fashion to anyone used to watching efficient violence on television. Tom spun back into the room, grabbed Mr Skerritt, who was uppermost, hooked one arm around him, and hauled him roughly away from Marriott Carswell, shouting, 'Come on! Stop! That's more than enough!' Marriott rolled over and then slowly got to his feet, brushing himself down. He was shaking – but not with fear. When he looked up, they could see he was laughing.

'Oh Canary! Canary!' he said. 'I could have you for assault. I was as nice as pie, wasn't I, Tom? I only came here to reassure him, didn't I? You're my witness.'

'Talk it over tomorrow,' said Tom, looking uncomfortable, for everything Marriott said was true and false at the same time. 'Unless you want to make some sort of definite charge,' he added in an official voice.

'Well, I do have the law as my witness, don't I?' Marriott Carswell repeated, stroking the side of his face as he turned to leave, grinning on and on, in spite of the graze. 'And I'll think about that charge tomorrow, Canary.' It seemed as if he really was going at last, but then he stopped in the doorway and turned back into the sitting room. 'And do you know why I'm even bothering to think? Because I had a sudden vision as I hit the doorframe back there. I might be semi-retiring, you know. Coming back home to settle down for a while. So I'm going to apply for permission to build a big holiday home for myself on the south side of Kaitangata, a little palace of a place, Spanish–American style. Terracotta, dusky pink, maybe – you'll love it. And you'll get a great view of it from here, too. Hey, we'll be able to watch one another boating and swimming – shout across to one another, wave . . .' He waved his hand at them all. It was a simple wave, but the smile behind it made it extremely unpleasant. 'So just apologise, and then we can put this behind us and work our way towards being good neighbours.' He waited, grinning, grinning, looking not at Mr Skerritt, but over at Mrs Skerritt and Kate.

Mr Skerritt was silent. His lips were so tightly folded together they looked more like a ruled line under his nose than a proper mouth.

Marriott Carswell sighed. 'OK! Have it your way! Don't worry about seeing me out.' He took out a handkerchief and dabbed at his cheek once more. His voice grew louder and more confident. 'Just coming, Tom! Sorry about that, but hey, it's just a graze. Anyway,' he was saying as he vanished into the hall, 'I need to get down to the boathouse. I'm late, late, late as it is, and–'

The front door closed, cutting off his last words.

21

Meredith's mother came to kiss her goodnight.

'We'll work our way through this,' she said, talking as much to herself as she was to Meredith. 'Oh dear! It's all such a mix-up between present things and past ones. With some people, nothing's ever over and done with.'

'Aren't you worried? About Dad and Kate? And Kaitangata?'

'Well, it's my job to worry, not yours,' Mrs Skerritt said. 'And I've had a lot of good worrying practice. But I'll have to rush off now and comfort your poor old dad. And Kate too, probably.'

Meredith's thoughts slid on past her father, and the strange battering Marriott Carswell had given him without striking a single blow.

'Do you think he really will build a house on the island?' she said. 'Mum, he's horrible. I love Kaitangata.

I don't want his terracotta terror cottage there.'

'Hey!' said Mrs Skerritt softly. 'Leave the word-twisting to Rufus. Anyhow even if old Marriott did build a terror cottage we'd find a way to get our own back . . . put up new water tanks, paint them purple and then stick big advertisements for herbal remedies on them.'

'Or Kate could spray insulting anti-Marriott slogans on them,' said Meredith, briefly entertained with this idea. 'And Rufus could think of something good.'

Mrs Skerritt smiled and got up.

'Kate!' she said. 'What an idiot! Spraying insults on Marriott's notices. Funny way of being a warrior!'

'Mum,' said Meredith. 'Mum! Marriott's going to *ruin* Kaitangata, isn't he, just for the fun of it? He's going to make it into something we hate. He's rich enough to do something like that, isn't he?'

Mrs Skerritt was silent. Then she sighed.

'Could be!' she said. 'Right now, he's probably just having us on. But somewhere along the line, *someone* will probably want to build on Kaitangata. A lot of people would like the idea of a holiday house on an island.'

'Mum, Kaitangata's my special place,' cried Meredith. 'I don't want it changed.'

Mrs Skerritt glanced at the door. Voices came up from below.

'Well, you never know,' she said. She was not answering Meredith but chasing some thought of her own. 'You know, Merry, sometimes it seems to me that . . .' she hesitated. 'Well, it just may be that the time has come for us to move on.' Saying this, Mrs Skerritt stared out into space, as if testing the words, hearing how they sounded in the outside air.

'Move on!' cried Meredith. She had been lying down, but now she bounced up again. 'You mean – leave the bay?'

'Well, people do move on,' said Mrs Skerritt. 'It *is* going to change around here, in ways we don't want it to change. It was bound to happen sooner or later, since we're so close to the city. And I don't want to spend the rest of my life eyeball to eyeball with Marriott . . . certainly not if he ever builds a terror cottage of any kind on Kaitangata. I mean, imagine him lying back on some balcony with a gin and tonic and field glasses like yours, peering in at us here. I know we can peer right back, but he'd probably enjoy it, whereas your dad and me – we just want to look out at the world, taking it all in, in a simple way. And a landscape gardener can always find work in other places, and there *are* a lot of other beautiful places in the country.'

'But Mum . . .' Meredith struggled with this horrifying idea. She flopped back on her pillow. 'What we need is a powerful enchantress,' she cried at last. 'Someone with power who could put a spell on Marriott.' And, as she spoke, a strange thought came into her head, running round and round inside her like a mouse on a pet-shop wheel. It was not a thought she could share with anyone, for it had wickedness hidden in it, and Meredith did not want anyone to know just how wicked she could be, even if it was only in her dreams.

'Look, I just have to go and be kind to your father,' her mother said. 'He's hating himself for losing his cool, and actually hitting out at Marriott. OK, so it's what he's wanted to do all year, but now he's done it he feels terrible. Because, funnily enough, it's turned him into a big loser. It's hard to be a violent man with anti-violent ideals. And then he's so strung up about Kate. *And* Kate's miserable about him. After all she *has* landed him right in it, hasn't she?'

'We're getting to be a dysfunctional family,' Meredith sighed aloud, secretly pleased with herself for remembering a word like 'dysfunctional'.

'The hell we are!' her mother exclaimed. 'We're great! We're tough! Having a few ups and downs is *part* of life. But goodnight, sleep tight, darling girl.'

Oddly enough, Meredith fell asleep almost at once.

At last the house grew quiet . . . then even quieter. A

velvet silence settled over it, as the moon, angling itself lower, laid a pale finger across Meredith's face. She stirred, as if she could feel its touch. Then, suddenly her eyes opened wide.

For a little while she lay gazing up dreamily through the shaft of light into the shadows that hovered under her ceiling. And then, slowly, very slowly, she climbed out of bed. She pulled a flat cardboard carton from under her bed and took out the little box, that looked black but was really blue. Meredith opened it; the moonlight shone on the silver ring that Marriott Carswell had once given to her mother. Taking it out of its blue box, she put it on her own finger and slid over to the window (walking a little unevenly like a doll answering the tug of invisible strings). Then, staring out into the shining night, she held out her ringed hand to the moon.

The bay from this angle was oval-shaped, and Kaitangata, like the dark pupil of a silver eye, seemed to stare back at her. The fist of the island, both dark and bright, struck upwards into the shiny air. From further round the bay, Trident Cove winked at Meredith, who winked back, oh so slowly – so very slowly – that she seemed to be taking her time from a clock in some other world. If she had glanced to her right, perhaps she would have seen a faint, yellowish glow filtering up from Marriott

Carswell's boathouse, where he was obviously still working in that office tucked in behind his boats. Perhaps he was touching the graze on the side of his face from time to time and laughing to himself.

'I'll help you,' she promised the island aloud, nodding as she promised. 'No terror cottages for you.' She held her hand with the ring on it still higher. 'Silver to silver,' she said at last, hissing the words into the night air. 'Marriott Carswell . . . Marriott Carswell . . . Marriott Carswell. I call you! I call you! I call you!' The strange voice that came out of her mouth was a sandy, gravelly voice that sounded as if it sifted out into the world through moss and fern roots. She took a deep breath. 'Kaitangata! Kaitangata! Kaitangata!' she whispered.

Then she dropped her arm and stared out to sea again. Nothing changed. Meredith stood there, silent now, staring and staring towards the island until a distant sound broke the stillness. Somewhere on the long beach below, in spite of the late hour, someone had started an outboard motor. Immediately Meredith turned, and, though all lights were out in the house and there was no way the moon could shine on the stairs, she made her way down to the front door, walking without the slightest stumble. The door was locked on the inside, but the key was still in the lock. She turned it, opened the door and moved on out into the night. Once across the verandah she paused and whistled soundlessly. But though her whistle was nothing more than the pursing of her lips, the laundry door opened behind her, and Pudding and Pie followed Meredith unobtrusively as she walked across the lawn, making for the End of the World.

21

Weaving her way now right, now left, Meredith found her way unerringly down the Zigzag with Pudding shooting ahead and arriving at the boathouse first, while Pie scuffled so closely around Meredith's feet she had to be careful not to trip. One after the other, Meredith and the two dogs stepped from the shadow of trees into a different world. The moon seemed to have disappeared. There were no stars in the arching darkness overhead, and yet the air seemed polished by that brassy light, almost like a dark sunlight but without warmth or welcome. It oozed to meet her, out of the sand, perhaps, or out of the air itself, touching everything with its nightmare gloss. Arriving at the boathouse, Meredith hooked her fingers through the loop of rope at the prow of the blue canoe, and pulled – quickly! quickly! Her family might be at her heels, and she must be on her own – must give herself freely to a world in which she would be nobody's daughter, nobody's sister, just her true, single inside self – Meredith the enchantress. *Just me!* Meredith found herself thinking, *Just the dogs, the blue canoe and me.* The canoe seemed to flinch and pull back like a third, unwilling dog, but Meredith was too strong. It surrendered at last, slid obediently across the sand, and into the shallow water.

Dreamily buckling on her lifejacket, she watched the tide coming in. A little wave ran towards her, carrying something on its back. A hand? No – of course not! Another rubber glove! The wave laid it on the sand, then seemed to vanish in two directions at once, running back towards the sea, but sinking down into the sand at the same time. The glove was left lying on its back, fingers curving slightly upward as if asking for something. Meredith waved at it, lying there, and thought the fingers flexed in answer.

'I know I'm dreaming,' Meredith thought. 'I know I'm dreaming, but this time the dream is doing what I tell it to do.'

So she climbed into the blue canoe and paddled out into the advancing water.

Pie sat in the prow of the canoe, while Pudding swam beside it, and Meredith was pleased to have the two dogs with her. She was alone, and yet she had company.

They landed at Shelly Beach. Pie hesitated, then leaped out, but without his usual eagerness, while Pudding came churning after them. Both dogs looked reluctant but resigned as they stood on the beach, Pudding shaking the water out of her woolly coat. As for Meredith, though she was frightened it was a different fear from the fear of other dream-visits, for this time she had deliberately chosen the fear. Walking towards the prow of the island, ignoring the mist that crept behind her from the west, she went from one little beach to another, nodding at the wet sand, and the undecipherable sentence the tide had written across it. The two dogs trotted just ahead of her, instead of casting backwards and forwards as they usually did, and the mist followed at her heels. There lay the skeleton of the fish, there lay the yellow glove and – yes again – there the sodden black sandal: spells set down in signs, spells which might counter that other spell, the one engraved by bulldozers on the hill above her home.

Meredith rounded the eastern end of the island and, carefully, looked ahead of her. The two dogs stayed beside her, seeing not smelling, calm and careful, too. Meredith read the sign beside the first beach, and thought she could feel the dogs reading with her. White printing on blue ... HAND BEACH. The sign on the beach beyond, which she already knew would say EYE BEACH, gleamed in the strange light. In the distance, on the third headland, she saw the gleam of a third sign, and made out yet again that host of nameless shadows with the smaller shadow standing in front of them. 'OK, let's get on with it,' she said to the dogs.

Once again Meredith leaped sideways as the raw pink hand grabbed at her ankle, but though she was terrified, it was by now an old, familiar terror, something to be lived and leaped through. She had no choice. The dream was like a tunnel, caving in behind her as she moved on through it. There was no turning back from this journey.

So, moving on through that brassy light, familiar now yet always strange, she avoided the hands, and ignored the great eye that opened in the little cliff beside the second beach to watch her go by. No way could she outstare Kaitangata. At last she scrambled across rocks and onto the third beach. MOUTH BEACH said the sign. Tethered to the sign was a boat she had seen before.

'Surprise, surprise!' said a voice.

She looked up. Marriott Carswell was grinning at her, from above the tideline. The brassy light edged in on him from all directions and he looked like an actor on a sandy stage.

'But why you?' he said. 'Where's your sister?'

'My sister?' repeated Meredith.

'I thought it must be your sister when I got the call.'

'What call?' asked Meredith.

'On my mobile!' he said, then stopped and frowned as if he weren't quite sure of what he was saying. 'Mind you, the reception isn't great on this side of the hill.' He quickly overcame his moment of uncertainty. 'Anyhow, what on earth are you doing here at this time of night? Isn't it a bit dangerous for you to be paddling around in the dark?'

'More dangerous for you,' said Meredith, feeling, strangely, that she was not using her own voice. Something had chosen her and was speaking through her.

'Oh, I've got nothing to worry about.' Marriot's expression was – not frightened, but somehow rather defensive. 'I know the harbour like the back of my hand. And this island is mine – *mine*, d'ye hear? Your family will never forget it's mine, because I meant what I said earlier. I'm going to build a holiday home here, and I'm going to sit on my verandah with my telescope, looking into your back yard and through your windows whenever the fancy takes me. As for you, you can just paddle back home again. I don't want to see any of you Skerritts on Kaitangata ever again.'

Meredith looked out to sea. A wave, not much more than a frill of foam and water on the very edge of the ocean, splashed lightly onto the sand, but there were no words hidden in this sound. The sea had nothing to say for itself.

'Anyhow, what's wrong with what I've done over there?' asked Marriott Carswell, pointing in the direction of Trident Cove. 'There was nothing there before – nothing! No great stands of rimu. No heritage-listed rainforests. The slopes were eroding. The farmers were struggling. Most of them were bloody thrilled to sell, I can tell you that. Couldn't wait. Same on this side of the bay. You ask the Pontys how they feel about it. Slogging their guts out for years, just to break even.'

Meredith stayed silent. She found she was waiting for something.

'As for that sister of yours, well, she's got problems, that's all I can say,' Marriott Carswell went on. 'Your dad should spend more time worrying about his own back yard, and less time worrying about mine.'

'He just wants things to stay beautiful,' said Meredith speaking at last. 'The way it was when he was a kid.'

'Beautiful?' exclaimed Marriott Carswell incredulously. 'He thought it was the bloody backside of the world when he was a kid, and so did I. I hated this blasted place. And it's worse now ... filled up with middle-class whingers who want the world to stay *pretty* just so they get a nice view from their picture windows. And what's wrong with a speedboat or two – or jet-skis? Sure they're a bit noisy, but people have *fun* with them. Gag your donkeys before you start raving on about jet-skis. But your old man has always thought his views were the only ones. He's always been a real pain in the you-know-what.'

Meredith could see that Marriott Carswell's hurt was an old one, running back into the past like a muscle of pain, which twitched every now and then. Back then he had been a loser, and he couldn't stand the memory of losing.

'As for your mum,' said Marriott Carswell, as if Meredith had mentioned her mother, 'did she ever tell you that she and I were quite an item before your dad came dancing back from overseas, acting like a great international know-all. *Quite an item*,' he repeated with emphasis. 'If he'd come back six months later I reckon you'd be my kid. And you'd be going to a decent school – St Anne's or one of those – and you'd have ponies and horses, not bloody donkeys.'

He looked around the beach, then over at Meredith. 'As for this island – can you honestly say you *like* it? Be honest . . . if a Skerritt can be honest, that is.' Though he was looking at Meredith as he spoke, she could tell he was really arguing with himself, about past injuries that still infuriated him.

Meredith thought about Kaitangata. She thought about walking around the shore, reading the various tales written there by the sea. She thought of the thrift springing from cracks in the rocks, the tough, tangled gorse and broom, the foxgloves, the pimpernels, and the heavy grasses bowed with last night's rain. She thought of the larks, singing high, wandering songs with no beginning or end, and the watchful, pacing seagulls. She thought of the clear water and the scuttling crabs leading busy, scavenging lives of their own, and seemed to feel the grains of dream sand suddenly stir and transform into a thousand scintillations. She felt the island inside her as well as outside.

'I don't just like it, I *love* it,' she said, speaking at last.

'*Love* it?' cried Marriott Carswell, wrinkling his face incredulously. 'Bullshit! It's a *nothing* place. But I'm going to burn off the gorse and broom, level some of the rough bits, spray it, plant a few nice English trees . . . not oaks, but poplars and willows, say. They take off quickly. Build a bridge to the mainland one day. And I'll have that holiday home right up high, just below the rocks so I can look out to the mouth of the harbour. Believe me, even if I'm not living here myself, someone else will want to. And you Skerritts will have my subdivision behind you, and – and some other place of mine in front of you.'

Meredith looked up to where she knew the island's rocky fist clenched itself against the sky. 'I like it *wild*!' she cried, punching upwards in a freedom sign of her own. And the island answered her. Meredith saw a ripple, not out in the sea, but right between her feet, rising and falling under the sand. Solid ground suddenly seemed to be nothing but a flapping picnic blanket with a spirit moving below it. A second, writhing ripple swept down the beach towards them. Marriott Carswell rocked from one foot to the other.

'The Twitch!' he exclaimed, and for the second time that evening Meredith saw him fall over, though this time there was no one actually hitting him. 'Kaitangata Twitch!' he was shouting as he pitched forward, this time onto his knees.

The strange feeling that the world was simultaneously straining in two different directions surged under Meredith's own feet, while Pudding raced south and Pie slid north, both barking hysterically. Then it was all over. It had taken less than a second.

But it wasn't over. Something had happened – was still happening. The bank behind Marriott Carswell was moving. Crumbs of dry earth began rolling, clods of clay pitched themselves forward like greyish-yellow dolls' heads, withered and misshapen and wearing wigs of grass. Then a whole slab of the bank began to topple down onto the beach. Marriott Carswell scrambled towards her on all fours, shouting as he did so.

Where the bank had been, an arched hole suddenly gaped at them. Torn moss hung down in shreds from its upper lip. The ribbed, upper inside surface of the new cave reminded Meredith of something that terrified her. She wanted to run away, but she couldn't. She had to watch. In this dream it was part of her job to be a witness.

'Oh God, look at that!' said Marriott Carswell wonderingly, talking more to himself than to her. 'An underrunner like – like a bloody *throat*. That roof's like the roof of a *mouth*.'

He stood up and, half-stooping, moved towards it.

'Be careful,' Meredith said in a wavering voice. After all, she must warn him. He must have his chance.

Marriott turned his head. She saw his teeth gleam, but he wasn't smiling.

'No Skerritt tells me where I can go on my own land,' he said.

He bent to peer into the newly revealed cave. Brassy dream-light fingered fern roots dangling from its ridged roof. Further back, that dream-light was swallowed by blackness.

And as Marriott peered into the cave, something moved out of the darkness, coming up through the throat and out of the mouth, changing shape as it came.

In the beginning, when it was at the very back of the throat, it seemed to be a host of people – it seemed to have many heads and many faces. The closer it came, the more it took a shape that Meredith recognised. It shrank, tightened, coloured up, until at last it stood in front of them . . . a little girl, wearing old-fashioned clothes, stiff as a white-headed doll, carrying a bouquet of flowers, and looking as if she were posing, right there in Kaitangata's greedy mouth, for a birthday photograph. Both dogs set up a savage barking, then leaped in front of Meredith, pointing their noses at the figure of the girl, who did not move but simply smiled on.

'What *is* this?' asked Marriott Carswell, suddenly frightened and furious with his own fear. 'Who set this up? What are you kids playing at?' He glared at Meredith.

Meredith saw that the fair-headed child was not quite right. As she stood looking out at them, her face puffed out on one side, and was then pulled back into line again. Her right eye swelled, and became a giant eye, mashing her nose to the left. But then, as if by some effort of will, she brought it all back into balance. One of her pale hands darkened as if it were bruising or rotting. All the time, she was looking past Marriott to Meredith. *Flick!* Meredith felt something twitch in her, as if the island was reeling her in.

'You don't frighten me with this act,' yelled Marriott Carswell. He lunged toward the strange child, right into that ridged mouth.

Meredith knew he was seizing, not a child, but Kaitangata itself. She knew he was suddenly feeling, there between his angry hands, the weight of it all – grass, gorse, headlands, tide lines, and even that rocky fist. It was the island itself he was pulling down around him.

'*Don't!*' she screamed, warning him – warning him even though she had, perhaps, led him into the island's power. 'Let it go! Let it go!'

But Marriott Carswell would not let go. Perhaps he could not. Kaitangata embraced him, transforming, as it did so, from pale past child into a dark, muscular lash – a tongue, perhaps – while the great upper lip of the cave protruded above him. Marriott Carswell glanced up . . . stopped shouting . . . began screaming hoarsely, desperately, as Kaitangata swallowed him. Meredith fell flat on the sand and rolled over, hiding her face in her arms and screaming, too.

The noise seemed to dissolve everything. Even time itself splintered. And no matter how loudly she cried out herself, she could still hear Marriott Carswell's terrified shrieks ringing inside her head, echoing now as if they were ringing somewhere in the deep heart of the island.

The horrified howling stopped. It stopped so sharply that the silence was like a blow. Meredith felt cold water soaking through her clothes and stroking her skin. The Kaitangata Twitch seemed to be rocking her again, but evenly now – on and on and on. It no longer felt like an earthquake. At last, the silence was broken by a familiar sound – the barking of dogs anxious for attention. The world beneath her hip and hands seemed to harden and take on some other form. Meredith turned her head.

Everything had changed. She was lying in the bottom of the blue canoe, and the light that surrounded her was not the brazen light of her dreams, but ordinary moonlight, strange as moonlight always is and yet familiar – the very moonlight that had lured her out earlier in the evening. The moon was about to vanish behind the hills on the far side of the bay, but the surface of the water was so bright it was easy to see everything around her. In front of her sat Pie, looking alert, while Pudding peered over the side of the canoe, wagging her tail. Meredith was on Kaitangata, but on the southern shore, not the northern. She was on Shelly Beach. She must have wandered down the Zigzag in her sleep, put on her lifejacket and actually canoed across the narrow band of sea, dreaming all the way. She had journeyed in her sleep, but now she was awake . . . wasn't she?

22

There was a soft, treading sound, shoes on sand.

'Don't worry!' a voice called softly out of the shadows. 'It's only me.' It was Lee Kaa padding up Shelly Beach towards her, as if he already knew all about her dreaming, and (maybe) just what to do about it. 'There I was, wandering along, taking a midnight moonlight walk of my own, and I saw you taking off,' he said. 'I borrowed one of your canoes and took off after you.' He pointed to the beach beside her, and Meredith saw the green canoe drawn up beside the blue one. 'I did call out to you once or twice, but you didn't answer. Thought you looked a bit strange somehow! Driven or maybe drawn! Now, how about I give you an escort home?'

Meredith nodded.

'OK, then!' said Lee, feeling in his jacket pockets. He took some cord from one pocket, and a little torch from the other.

'You never know when you're going to need light or string,' he said. 'Just hold the torch for me.'

Then, as Meredith held the light in a shivering hand, he looped the two canoes together.

'We'll both get into the blue one,' he said, 'that's the biggest, isn't it? Paddle home in style?' Lee climbed in behind Meredith, treating her as delicately as if she were made of sea foam, then picked the paddle out of the sea. Pudding scrambled in behind Lee, while Pie stood, like a sort of figurehead in the front.

'I think I've killed Marriott Carswell,' said Meredith. Words and tears tumbled out of her. She found she was trembling violently, and clenched her hands together, trying to hold herself still.

Lee stopped pushing the canoe out into the sea.

'Where was this?' he asked.

'On the other side of the island,' she said, shivering. 'Kaitangata opened its mouth and swallowed him.'

'Ha!' said Lee, but it was more a sigh than a laugh. He was silent for a moment, then he said, 'There's no way you could have done that, because I've had you in full sight ever since I saw you setting out. You haven't been round to the other side of the island. You only landed here about five minutes ago.'

'But I called him,' Meredith mumbled. 'I called him

and he came. And the island ate him.' Somewhere behind her ribs, her stomach muscles tightened and heaved. It was as if the Kaitangata twitch had actually become part of her. Meredith looked away, struggling and clenching her teeth. She felt torn between fear of Kaitangata and fear of herself because of what she might have done. Marriott Carswell might have been a villain, but she did not want to be the one who had lured him into the dreadful mouth of Kaitangata.

'Ha,' Lee Kaa was saying again. 'Is that right?' The paddle dipped; behind them the moon dipped too, grazing the edge of the hills; the air darkened. 'Fifty years back,' said Lee, leaning forward, and speaking over Meredith's shoulder, 'I was a kid like you. A kid who dreamed. Now, my people – they're your people too, come to think of it – they've kept clear of Kaitangata. Like I told you back a bit, it was – well, sort of *tapu*. A forbidden place. People had been taken there in the old times to be killed and eaten. That's history. But when I was round about your age, maybe a bit younger, I thought I was beyond all that old Maori stuff – too clever for it. I used to row across and wander all round the island. And that's when my dreams became special in a way. Not all the time, just every now and then!' Lee was paddling in a dreamy way. 'I know you need to get home,' he said, a little apologetically, 'but maybe I've got something to tell you that nobody else can tell. OK?'

'OK!' said Meredith, for Lee's words were bringing the beginning of relief with them. Her twitching stomach had quietened down. She was glad to think she might not be the only dreamer of sinister island dreams.

'The Gentrys!' Lee exclaimed softly. 'They had this plan, you know. They were going to build a boarding house on the island – offer people an island holiday. I don't reckon it would ever have caught on, but that's what they were planning to do. Access by barge, can you believe it? Of course, once Shelly disappeared they gave up on all that, and nobody remembers that plan these days. But the thing is – I had this dream, and since then I've always felt it might have been my fault – Shelly disappearing, I mean.'

'Were you at her birthday party?' asked Meredith.

'Oh no. The Gentrys would never have asked *me*,' said Lee. 'I was a Maori kid from round the bay. No, what happened was I went to sleep out in the sun, and dreamed myself into that party. I dreamed that I climbed the track up to the top of the island, and that Shelly followed me, holding a dirty great bunch of flowers someone must have given her. And I dreamed that I was going to climb the rocks at the top of the island, but she said she was going to climb them first, because the island was hers, not mine. And the thing was, in my dream, I *knew* that she'd do that. I knew she was a pushy kid, and that telling her what I was going to do was a bit like daring her to do it first. So, up she went and I followed her. And I dreamed that while she was up there, the rocks somehow unfolded . . . rose up pointing to the sky like fingers, and then clenched down on her. Terrible! But it was only a bad dream. I woke up, yelling, back in my own garden, with my own mum rushing to see what was wrong with me.'

'But Shelly *did* disappear,' said Meredith. 'Do you really think she was caught in the hand of the island?'

'How do I know?' said Lee Kaa. 'Something happened, sure, and she disappeared, sure, but I reckon my dream was only the *sign* of it, not the thing itself. Look, they turned over every stone on that island. They'd have found her if she'd been caught in the rocks. See, my *theory* is that the island found a way into me when I was asleep, sort of plugged into me, like someone might plug a heater or a drill into some point where energy would flow, and I think it used the sort of energy it found in me, in my – my . . . let's say my dreaming, to set something going in the world around it – to protect itself. Because it needed protection. Maybe the spilled blood of the old people, hundreds of years back, gave it the power to do that.' He paused. 'I think it *is* haunted,' he said at last. 'Haunted by history. So what? History haunts all human places.'

By now they were quite close to the home beach, paddling in darkness, for the moon had at last disappeared and now only the stars were shining out. Scorpio was setting but Meredith knew that Orion, belted and armed, would be striding up out of the east, bringing summer with him. She sat thinking about what Lee had just told her.

'I love Kaitangata,' she said. 'Well, I used to love it.' She tested her feeling like someone gingerly feeling a bruise. 'I think I still do.'

Lee stared up at the stars, leaning back on his oars.

'I don't know if I love it or not,' he said. 'I do know that it is like – like part of me by now. Part of my world ever since I can remember. That's why I play to it at night on my saxophone. I feel it listening to me.' He broke off and shrugged. 'And who knows? Marriott may show up tomorrow, sharp and nasty as ever.'

'Do you really think he will?' asked Meredith, and listened to the silence behind her.

'No,' said Lee at last. 'Between you and me, I think he's met his match. I reckon Kaitangata – I think it . . . it *protects* itself by feeding on dreams. I reckon it's been feeding on yours. But hey! I could be wrong.'

'Is it a wicked island?' asked Meredith, as they pulled the canoe up to the Skerritt boathouse.

'No way!' said Lee, stepping through the shallows. He took out his little torch, and turned it on, so that it pointed up the path with a thin finger of light. 'Wicked? Good? That's *people*-talk. Kaitangata is something older than people. Beyond them. Now just you think of all the things people do to land – clear it, cut it, bruise it, burn it. They smash it around, smooth it down, and all to suit themselves. I reckon that, every now and then, there are a few pieces that want to stay the way they are – maybe get their own back, even. And Kaitangata's one of those pieces. It makes itself powerful by feeding on – well, whatever offers itself. And maybe Marriott offered himself.'

'It's so spooky,' said Meredith, and began to cry. Lee helped her out onto the sand and then patted her shoulder.

'It's the way things are,' he said. 'You already know that. Everything gives up one shape, sooner or later, and takes on another. Once you get used to the idea, it seems halfway beautiful. Well, it does to me. The game of changes I call it, and at my time of life I'm edging towards a big change myself. And now I'd better get you home. Will your parents be offering a reward, do you reckon?'

'A million dollars,' said Meredith, smiling through tears. 'But they'll have to pay in little lots over a thousand years.'

'Oh well, that should keep me in beer,' said Lee Kaa. They climbed the Zigzag, and crossed the lawn, turning their backs on the End of the World. Lee knocked on the door, and after a moment there was the sound of anxious feet, thudding down the stairs. A few minutes after that, Meredith was being exclaimed over, hugged, kissed, warmed and given midnight treats, an island no longer, but part of her family, as she always had been, and always would be, for in the game of changes there were a few happy things that would never really change.

23

'I'm going to have to swallow my pride,' Mr Skerritt told Kate at breakfast the next day. 'Do you realise that? I am going to have to apologise. To Marriott,' he added. It was the first time Meredith had heard her father refer to his enemy without playing with his name in a thumping way. *Marriott Cars*-well . . . three blows and a grunt! Simply calling him 'Marriott' made him seem too much like an old friend. 'The dreadful thing is – he deserves an apology from both of us.'

'Don't you dare apologise!' yelled Kate. Her stubble seemed to bristle all over her round head. 'He set you up. He wanted you to hit him. He tempted you. And you fell for it.'

'*He* fell for it,' said Rufus but everyone ignored Rufus.

'You may be right,' sighed Mr Skerritt. 'It doesn't let me off the hook, though, does it?'

He rang first Marriott Carswell's home and then his office, only to be told that Mr Carswell was not currently available. He was given a mobile number, which he rang, but the call did not go through. And when he rang again, late in the afternoon, he was told that Mr Carswell had left town. He had been unexpectedly called to Sydney, and no one was sure when he would be back. The voices on the other end of the phone gave nothing away but almost at once a curious, creeping gossip began inching around the bay. There was some business problem that nobody seemed sure about. Mr Carswell was not answering any calls – even his mobile had fallen silent.

That evening Mrs Hansen from the pub at the head of the harbour rang about someone who might want to buy a donkey. She said almost as an afterthought, 'Doesn't look too good for Marriott Carswell, does it?' Mrs Skerritt asked, cautiously, what she meant.

'It was on the news tonight. Seems he's had some sort of financial crash,' Mrs Hansen explained. 'Right out of the blue! Bang! Sounds like a big one. Some other big international company – Idiot Industries or something – has sort of come down on him and swallowed him up. And it looks as if he owes a lot of money. It even sounded as if he might be declared bankrupt. Watch this space, eh?'

'Idiot Industries!' cried Rufus indignantly. 'I said that first.'

'Good name for them,' exclaimed Mr Skerritt. 'But it'll probably be that lot we've heard of ... Eyot Holdings. Aren't they the ones who ...' His voice faded as he followed Mrs Skerritt into another room.

'Eyot Industries,' Meredith repeated in a soft voice filled with a sudden, secret puzzle. 'Eyot! A small island!' she remembered. And she looked out of the window at Kaitangata, stretching itself calmly as the tide came in. Maybe an island like Kaitangata could reach out and connect with other islands. Maybe there was more than one way of being swallowed.

The following morning even some of the minibus kids were talking about it. Marriott Carswell's whole great business suddenly seemed to have come crashing down on him.

Ideas and guesses filled the air. Meredith listened – listened, but said nothing. Sometimes it seemed to her that the right sort of dream might link into the world and shift things around, though mostly she began thinking it was all a strange sort of accident ... nothing to do with her father or even with her. Yet Lee Kaa was right. Kaitangata had been threatened. It had wakened; it had stolen her dreams. And perhaps, in some mysterious way, it had used the power of her dreams to save itself.

At home the topic of Marriott Carswell kept on coming up. 'He's run away,' said Mr Skerritt. 'Chickened out.'

'He didn't sound as if he was chickening when he last spoke to us,' said Mrs Skerritt doubtfully. 'But there's no doubt about it. He's been swallowed up by someone even bigger than he was. Otherwise he'd be back here, being rich and powerful all over the place.'

'I'll bet he was setting out to do a drug deal somewhere and the FBI or someone caught onto him,' said Kate, speaking of Marriott as if he were history already. 'He was that sort of man.'

'So! Is the bay saved yet?' Rufus asked his parents, but neither of them replied.

Of course, as it turned out, Marriott's plans were not his alone. They had become an official District Scheme, and strangers – part of a New Zealand company associated with the mysterious Eyot Holdings, people who had never visited the bay before – suddenly appeared and began carrying on with Marriott's work. People who had already bought sections began to build the very houses Mr Skerritt had foretold – big, expensive houses with huge foundations dug deep into the hillside. One family camped on their section in the weekends.

Unexpectedly Meredith made friends with Martin, the boy of this family, a reader who knew *The Lord of the Rings* almost by heart and carried books of ghost stories around with him. Many of the new families needed help when it came to working out their garden, and suddenly Mr Skerritt had a lot of local work, which he enjoyed. As for the fight with the Pontys – there seemed to be no more reason for it. Allan and Rufus began hanging out together once more. Sharon invited Meredith to her birthday party, and Martin, Meredith and Sharon wandered along the beach together, searching for bits of green and blue glass which had been turned into smooth jewels by the tumbling of the sea on the stones.

The thrift began to bloom.

'You came with the thrift,' Mrs Skerritt said to Meredith as they strolled along the beach one evening. 'What do you want for your birthday this year?'

Meredith looked sideways at the island. It looked so small, so ordinary now. It was sleeping soundly, as she herself slept these days, with no chair under the door and no dressing-gown cord tying her to her bed. For some reason, she no longer had any fear of walking in her sleep, and though she was never totally sure if she was asleep or dreaming, she had stopped worrying about it. It was a question beyond all worry.

Her birthday came. Her family brought her a birthday breakfast in bed – pancakes and a rose in a silver vase. She was given books, and a coupon for a special sailing weekend put on by the new Trident Cove yacht club. And there was a letter from her grandparents, marked 'Not to be opened until your birthday'. Everyone else watched her curiously as she opened and read the card.

'Gran says Happy Birthday,' she read. 'They've both been going to cooking classes and Grandpa can make really good muffins. And . . . oh man! Hooray! Dad! Dad! They've bought one of the Wittwood sections.'

Everyone in the family cried out in a chorus of astonishment.

'Give me that!' said Mr Skerritt, snatching the card and reading rapidly. 'It's true. They're going to build a cottage and move back here. I can't believe it.'

'Ace!' cried Rufus. He looked gleeful and then, suddenly, puzzled. 'As if they were siding with you-know-who!'

'Rubbish,' said Mr Skerritt. 'It'll be wonderful to have them back again. Wonderful!'

'Sure! Sure!' said Rufus. 'But they wouldn't have been able to get back here again if there hadn't been that extra building space, would they? And we hate that.'

Mr Skerritt stood frowning. He looked right and left with a curious desperation, almost as if he was longing for some magical voice to speak out of the air and chant a spell that would allow everything to fall into place. There would be room for grandparents up on the hillside, but for no one else. And the grandparents would move in without changing anything. But at last he sighed. He shrugged. He flung out his arms helplessly and then let them flop down to his side.

'I don't know!' he cried. 'I just don't know. There's no *sense* in anything any more.'

Mrs Skerritt laughed and put her arm around his shoulders.

'Darling!' she said. 'Life's always been madder than we want it to be. We just have to do the best we can, moment to moment.'

Mr Skerritt shrugged again. Then at last he smiled.

'OK! Yes! Things are what they are,' he said. 'Let's just relax and enjoy them.'

'Right on!' Mrs Skerritt and Rufus said, almost together.

That afternoon, before Kate was home from school and while Rufus was busy playing computer games over at the Pontys', Meredith did something she had not done for weeks. She tucked a certain box under her arm, and set off down the Zigzag onto the beach. The dogs followed eagerly after her. A few yachts were already tacking across the bay, but she suddenly felt as solitary, as simple, as pure as she felt in winter when the harbour was empty and still. As she pulled out the blue canoe, she shivered, but it was a calm shiver, a shiver for the past not the present, for she knew she was not going to be in any danger.

Meredith landed at Shelly Beach. Everything she looked at seemed, in this mood, transformed. Each foxglove bell was outlined with a thread of – of something that seemed to Meredith like nothingness – a thin line of some different kind of space from the space that she herself belonged to. Every shell and blade of grass declared itself.

From the box in the bottom of the canoe she took out the great shell Lee Kaa had given her and began to walk along the beach, blowing softly into it. Its melancholy, mossy song somehow echoed back into itself as it sang out into the world. She flapped her hand over the wide mouth of the shell, and the sound rose and fell, rose and fell in musical waves matching the small sea waves that curled up softly before flopping on the sand. Holding the shell and blowing into it, Meredith walked along beaches and over rocks to the pointed top of the tear-shaped eyot that was Kaitangata. Then she wandered along Hand Beach, over more rocks, along Eye Beach and carefully across Mouth

Beach, without looking left or right. There were no notices to name the beaches. Well, there never had been. At the broad western end of the island, she leaped from rock to rock, hooting softly all the time, worked her way around the point of the island, and came back onto the sand once more. On and on until the blue canoe came into sight. She had marched almost all the way around Kaitangata, playing on her shell.

All the time, whether she was walking on sand or rock, she felt someone or perhaps something watching her, but she did not turn. In a way, she had been expecting to be watched. Both dogs began to whine softly, and press against her.

Bending, Meredith gave Pudding a loving pat.

'It's all right,' she said soothingly, putting the big shell on the sand. 'Everything's OK.' Pudding, still whining, stretched herself up in a half-leap, putting her paws on her shoulders, so Meredith took her paws and made her dance in a circle with her. As she danced she sang, inventing a few of her own words to an old song:

Hi-tiddly-hi-ti Island,
Everybody wears a smile.
Hi-tiddly-hi-ti Island,
Ev'rybody lives in style . . .

The life's so bright and swift and gay
You live two weeks then fade away,
For once you're called you have to stay
On Hi-tiddly-hi-ti Isle.

Looking over Pudding's woolly shoulder as they revolved, barking and singing in duet, she half-expected to glimpse Marriott Carswell even though she knew he had lost interest in this part of the world. Mouth Beach (in more than one place and more than one form) had swallowed its enemy. Meredith stopped dancing, released Pudding, and laid her hand on the nearest rock. It was rough with lichen and warm with sunlight, and she imagined it rising and falling under her hand as if the island were breathing. But, of course, dancing in a circle always made you dizzy.

'I don't want to change you,' she shouted aloud to whatever it was that was watching her. 'I want you to stay exactly as you are.' Then she picked up the shell again and took a breath to blow on it once more as she walked the last few yards to the canoe. Then, at last, she turned to look behind her, and found she was looking into a face. She had never seen it before, but all the same she recognised it.

That face was neither old nor young . . . neither male nor female. One eye was like a hollow, the other was like a rockpool alive at the edges with fine, waving weed. The nose reminded Meredith of a dried, twisted gorse stem. Or was it stone with lichen on it? Or even sand? Meredith made herself smile, and saw her own reflection, dark in its deep rockpool eye. Perhaps the curious face copied her smile. Afterwards, she was sure that she had seen teeth of broken shell, and a crab, creeping from the corner of the mouth and scrambling hastily across its cheek. The smile, if it was a smile, widened. Then the face closed its eyes, and Meredith closed hers too. She blew a last cloudy note, moving her left hand over the mouth of the shell. When she looked again the face had disappeared, though all the parts that had made it were still there . . . the bark, the stone, the hollow, the lichen, the dried gorse stem, the sand, the crab. Whatever had trusted her and shown itself in order to smile at her had fallen back into its separate pieces.

Meredith whistled to the dogs, and walked back to the blue canoe. Around her she felt the island changing – but changing in its own way and in its own time. She felt the thin soil shifting over the rocks, the thrift growing up through the gorse, becoming brighter as spring advanced. She put the great shell carefully back into its box and began to paddle home. Ahead of her she made out the donkeys in their donkey paddock, the jennies in a cluster with last year's foals among them. Glancing sideways, she couldn't help seeing the definite scarlet of the Carswell boathouse, now locked and unused, and further along the beach she saw the light reflected from Lee Kaa's glasshouses. Further up the hillsides, above the boathouse and the donkey paddock, wound the new road, with the foundations of soon-to-be houses on either side of it. In a few years, twenty or thirty, say (nothing much when you thought of the age of the hills), the people who lived there would have mostly become friends and neighbours. Her grandparents would be living there. They would wander down for cups of tea, she would wander up for Anzac biscuits and home-made icecream. For some reason, accepting that new road, even though it was signalling great alterations in the world of her childhood, made her feel somehow older and wiser. *Maybe this is my first day of being grown-up* she thought, paddling onwards.

Mixed world! Mixed world! Lee Kaa was walking by on the beach, and they waved to each other but he did not wait. Like Meredith, Lee Kaa liked to be on his own sometimes. *Dreamers do*, thought Meredith. *Dreams branch out when you're alone, and dreamers are all islands, really.* She reached their shabby boathouse, pulled the blue canoe into it, then, carefully carrying her shell and with the dogs on either side of her, Meredith ran for the

Zigzag, and scrambled back over the Edge of the World to her family and her birthday dinner, while behind her Kaitangata, wrapped in its own silence, lay like a tear on the smooth cheek of the bay.